The police had cordoned off the entire east dock and the onlookers were forced to stand up on park tables to get a glimpse of the corpse being lifted onto a gurney and slid into the back of a Kings Harbor ambulance. I was glad I'd been spared a first-hand look at Walter Trinidad's body, Jess's description having been enough to last me quite a while. I scanned the clusters of police officers who were mostly standing around talking and spotted Martha talking to a young woman.

"Cass, I'm glad you're here," she said. "This is Erica Trinidad. Erica, this is Cassidy James, the private investigator I told you about."

"Pleased to meet you. " She shook my hand with a firm, even grip.

"Erica," Martha went on, "is the niece of the recently deceased. She's been visiting for a few days on her way up North and finds herself in the unenviable position of being the only kin in the area. For the time being, we've asked her to stay in town and she's agreed, but she's anxious to get on her way and asked me if I knew of anyone in the private sector who might expedite the investigation. Naturally, I thought of you."

"I'm sorry, Ms. Trinidad," I said. "But I'm afraid my friend here has overstated my qualifications. I have no experience with murder cases, and if in fact that's what this turns out to be, I doubt I could be of much help. I'm sure the police will do everything they can to handle the situation expediously." I smiled sweetly at Martha, thinking "Touché!"

"Oh, it was murder all right," Erica said.

LOOKING FOR NAIAD?

Buy our books at
www.naiadpress.com

or call our toll-free number
1-800-533-1973

or by fax (24 hours a day)
1-850-539-9731

1ST IMPRESSIONS

A CASSIDY JAMES MYSTERY

KATE CALLOWAY

THE NAIAD PRESS, INC.
2000

Printed in the United States of America on acid-free paper
First Edition
Second Printing January, 1999
Third Printing February, 2000

Editor: Christine Cassidy
Cover designer: Bonnie Liss (Phoenix Graphics)
Typesetter: Sandi Stancil

Library of Congress Cataloging-in-Publication Data

Calloway, Kate. 1957–
    First impressions / by Kate Calloway.
        p.   cm.
    ISBN 1-56280-133-3 (pbk. : alk. paper)
    1. Private investigators—Oregon—Fiction.   2. Women
detectives—Oregon—Fiction.   3. Lesbians—Oregon—Fiction.
I. Title.
PS3553.A4245F57   1996
813'.54—dc20   95-51025
                                                                               CIP

For Carol,
the only inspiration I need.

About the Author

Kate Calloway was born in 1957. She lives in Southern California with her lover and two cats. A teacher by day, a poet by night, she is really just a song writer at heart. *First Impressions*, her first novel in the Cassidy James mystery series, has been followed by *Second Fiddle, Third Degree, Fourth Down, Fifth Wheel, Sixth Sense,* and *Seventh Heaven.*

Acknowledgments

Special thanks to the women who bravely read my first novel, offering insights and encouragement along the way. You were not only courageous, but terribly kind: Carol, Lyn, Donna, Carolyn, Linda, Paula, Murrell and Deva; true sisters all.

I'd also like to thank my family, whose unconditional love and support have always given me the space to grow and flourish.

Chapter One

The problem with dumping a body in Rainbow Lake is that it almost immediately rises to the top, even when weighted down with rope and cement. The blame lies with the catfish and giant sturgeon that feed along the weedy bottom, scavenging for food. Together they make very short work of any flesh drifting their way, and it isn't long before what's left bounces to the surface, presenting a grotesque discovery for some unlucky boater.

Walter Trinidad hadn't been under more than forty-eight hours before our mail carrier, Buddy

Drake, thumped over him on his morning route. Thinking he'd hit a floating log, Buddy, an adept boatsman, wheeled his dinged-up Bow Rider around so he could tie the log to his stern and later drag it up the bank of his lake-front home. A shrewd scavenger, Buddy had not needed to buy firewood or lumber for many years, living quite comfortably off what treasures the lake and land provided.

When he reached into the water to grasp his latest treasure, Buddy instead got a fistful of Walter Trinidad's thick red beard which the fish had left unscathed. It was that beard that helped identify Walter Trinidad, since the rest of his face was largely unrecognizable.

News probably travels faster in Cedar Hills, Oregon, than anywhere on earth. By the time I had showered, blow-dried my hair into a reasonably fashionable style and decked myself out in my old, gray sweats and tennies for my morning walk, Buddy Drake had already towed Walter Trinidad's body to the county dock.

I hopped into my boat, a sky blue, open-bow Sea Swirl, and motored the half mile to Cedar Hills Marina where I kept a slip. At full speed, the trip took only a few minutes, but often I took it slower, enjoying the smells, sights and sounds of life on the lake. That morning as I putt-putted along, I noticed the throng of townspeople gathered around the county dock, but I didn't stop, thinking vaguely that perhaps someone had bought a new boat that the locals were ogling. Tommy Green met me as I pulled up to the gas dock at the marina.

"Morning, Miz James. Didja hear the news?" he asked, an impish grin on his young, sunburned face.

"Hi, Tommy. What news is that?"

"Heck, ya passed right by it. Ol' Buddy Drake run over that Walter Trinidad 'bout an hour back."

"Buddy Drake ran him over? Is he all right?" I asked.

"You want I should fill this up for you?" Tommy indicated the gas pump. I nodded and he continued. "Nah, he was already kilt. Fish got him purdy bad too. Weren't much left of him from what I could see. I went right over as soon as I heard, but Mr. Townsend told me to come back and finish washin' off these ramps. Soon as I'm through, though, I'm headin' right back over. You wanna go?"

The prospect of seeing a partially eaten Walter Trinidad did not appeal to me in the least. In fact, I'd hardly liked looking at the man alive. Rude and overbearing, Walter Trinidad had made it big in California real estate, and bought himself a luxurious lake-front estate in Oregon, where he spent two months each summer lording it over the less fortunate townsfolk. I doubted that his demise would be mourned by many.

"I think I'll pass, Tommy. But thanks for the invite. I trust you'll fill me in on all the sordid details later."

"Be happy to do it, Miz James. My pleasure."

As usual, it was hard to know if Tommy was joking or serious. His elfin features made him seem always on the verge of laughter, and his bright eyes twinkled with perpetual mischief. His accent, though, was straight out of *Deliverance*. Half the time he sounded like a back woods hillbilly, but then he'd come up with a startling insight that made me think Tommy was a heck of a lot brighter than he let on.

3

Where he'd gotten his accent was a mystery. In fact, he wasn't the only Cedar Hills local who talked in a stylized twang that hinted of Texas, Alabama and the Ozarks all rolled into one. After three years of mixing with the locals, I still marveled at the rich and complex dialect that seemed to permeate the town. Ten miles south, in Kings Harbor, people talked in what was, to me, regular English. But here in Cedar Hills, a town of not quite nine hundred, at least half the citizenry spoke in what I humorously referred to as the Cedar Hills drawl.

I left my boat in Tommy's capable hands, hefted my trash bags into the dumpster provided for marina customers, then set off on my daily trek through the streets of Cedar Hills.

Living alone in a house accessible only by boat may seem like a hardship to some, but it's my kind of paradise. It's true, it takes longer to get groceries and take out the trash, but these minor incon-veniences are just part of the charm of living on the lake. My daily jaunt through Cedar Hills provides me with all the exercise and social life I need. I'm always happy to get back to my oak and cedar home with its open-beam ceilings, large, brick fireplace and picture windows overlooking the lake. My two cats, Gammon and Panic, are loyal and loving companions, and in the event I require some actual human interaction, I have my best friend Martha in Kings Harbor a quick phone call away.

For three years I've lived this way, healing from the loss of my lover who succumbed at last, in painful defeat, to cancer. She had been my life mate, my partner, my long-time companion. In the end,

4

reduced to a mere skeleton of herself, she begged to go, and I too prayed to a God I had long been cursing to hasten her death. When it was over, the silence she left behind was unbearable. What was left of my life held no meaning. The money from her substantial inheritance, her life insurance, and the properties we owned together were enough to tide me over indefinitely. I had no need, or desire, to continue my teaching career. I had no taste for the incessant sunshine of Southern California, which before had always been a pleasure. It's not that my will to live was gone, just my zest for living.

It was Martha, my first roommate in college, who talked me into coming to Oregon. She had been steadily working her way up the ranks of the Kings Harbor Police Department and positively glowed with enthusiasm for life in the Pacific Northwest.

"Cass, you gotta try it," she told me long distance, after Diane died. "The air is still blue, when it isn't raining, and the people actually say hello to one another. And," she added, her husky voice full of laughter, "none of the women have that anorexic unhealthiness they've got in California."

Martha, who has always battled her weight, had detested the bikini-clad sorority types that dotted the poolside of our dormitory at UCLA fifteen years ago. I could see how Oregon would suit her.

"The one bad thing is, " she went on, "you can't tell the dykes from the straights. I mean it, Cass. Every other woman you see is dressed in jeans and a flannel. It can be confusing."

"Must be quite a problem for you," I teased. Martha was somewhat famous for her amorous liaisons. "Hope you haven't made any errors in judgment. You used to brag that you could spot a lesbian a mile away."

"I damn near did, Cass. It was a narrow miss, I can tell you. I've had to learn to slow down some. Of course, I am getting older. Can't keep up with my own reputation, if you know what I mean."

As usual, my conversation with Martha left me laughing and feeling better. Several conversations later, Martha convinced me to come up for a visit, and by the time my visit was over, I had fallen in love with the nearby town of Cedar Hills. When I discovered the beautiful, natural wood house which sat perched above the lake in a clearing surrounded by cedar and fir, I knew I'd found my new home, my place for healing.

As I walked along that morning, stretching my legs, I chuckled over Martha's continual influence in my life. Not only had she been the one to introduce me to the lesbian lifestyle twelve years earlier, but she had rescued me from the doldrums of Southern California and shortly thereafter convinced me to try a new vocation, that of private investigator.

"You've got to be kidding!" I said when she first brought it up. "I don't know the first thing about that kind of stuff."

"But you're a natural, Cass. You've got all the right instincts. Listen, we've got detectives on the force who don't have half the inclination you do for this line of work. And the beauty of being a private investigator is you don't have to take a bunch of flak from the higher-ups. You can take a case or leave it. You can pick and choose. You're your own boss."

"But Martha," I said, secretly warming to the idea, "you're forgetting one very important fact. Basically, I'm a coward. Don't private investigators get shot at a lot?"

"Cass, you've been watching too much *Magnum P.I.* It's not really that dangerous. Most of the time it's using logic and determination to find solutions other people can't see. It's exactly what you did when I was having trouble on that Blake case, and you came up with the answer none of the rest of us could see. That's when I first got the idea that you're a natural. Besides, we could use a decent P.I. around here. The only one worth his salt is Jake Parcell, and he's pushing seventy. Anyway, what do you have to lose? If you don't like it, you can always go back to fishing off your dock."

The truth was, I was bored out of my mind and needed some kind of purpose for getting up in the morning. Two months of nothing but fishing was about all I could take. Finally, I let Martha introduce me to her friend Jake, a cranky old cuss who was an ex-cop turned private investigator in Kings Harbor. For the better part of three years I worked with Jake, learning the ropes, running his errands, doing his paperwork, and keeping him company on long, lonely stakeouts. The job was often boring, with stretches of no action at all. But just often enough to keep me interested, something really challenging would come along and I discovered, much to my own amazement, that I was actually a pretty good detective. My natural inclination toward nosiness seemed to lend itself to investigative work. In addition to thinking logically, I was extremely determined, and once I got started on something, I usually pursued it to completion. Even Jake, who rarely had a kind word for anyone, told me he thought I was a natural-born snoop. High praise, considering.

He paid me next to nothing, but what I gained from him, besides learning the ins and outs of being a P.I., was an impressive ability to pick locks and a fairly good notion of when someone was lying or telling the truth. I also learned enough old cop jokes and stories to last me a lifetime.

Martha taught me how to shoot a gun, and I became a fairly accurate shot on the firing range with my Smith & Wesson .38. I had at first balked at her insistence that I learn my way around firearms, but she convinced me that living alone in the woods, in a house with no access road, was reason enough to own and be able to handle a gun. In the unlikely event that I ever did find myself in a dangerous situation while doing detective work, she said, it would be an added bonus to have some form of self-protection.

So here I was, a thirty-year-old woman who could pick locks and handle a gun. If that wasn't enough to convince someone of my detective skills, well, I had a stack of fancy calling cards and a keen little license proving I was in fact a real detective. But in truth, now that I had actually gotten my license, I was thinking of canning the whole idea as a lark and going back to some serious trout fishing off my dock.

If someone had told me that morning, as I walked

myself into a sweat, that I would soon be working on a case involving the murder of Walter Trinidad, I wouldn't have believed them. But before I had finished my walk, I was indeed caught up in the whole affair.

Chapter Two

At the corner of the last leg of my daily route is the town's only store, McGregors, conveniently situated across from two of the three bars in town. For a town this small, McGregors is a surprisingly first-rate supermarket, and it was my plan to pick up an artichoke and a steak. That with some sautéed shiitake mushrooms and a good Cabernet would make a pretty decent dinner. Just because I lived alone didn't mean I had to dine on frozen TV dinners, and in the years since Diane's death I'd become something of a gourmet cook.

Before I could get through the parking lot, however, an aging, beat-up green Ford pickup came rumbling into the lot and pulled up alongside me. Jess Martin was hard to miss with his six-foot, two-inch frame and his long brown hair, which he wore tied back in a ponytail. He had a perpetual stubble of beard on his lean cheeks that gave him a devil-may-care appearance, and if he'd worn a patch over one eye, he'd have looked like a swashbuckling pirate. He seemed oblivious to his good looks, though, which was one reason I liked him. Like so many of Cedar Hills's inhabitants, Jess was a cast-off from another era. A latent hippie who'd done hard time in Vietnam, he had found a measure of peace in Cedar Hills, where he worked odd jobs for the rich lakehouse owners during the summer season. There were rumors about a dishonorable discharge and all sorts of speculation, but from what I'd seen, Jess was a stand-up guy with a heart of gold. And I'd learned not to place much stock in Cedar Hills gossip, anyway. He did odd jobs for me year-round and we had developed a close rapport.

"Well, there you are," he said through the open window of his truck. "Been looking all over for you. How's my favorite detective?"

"Hey, Jess. What's up?"

"Well, if you don't know, you're the only one in town who doesn't. Buddy Drake found a dead body in the lake this morning. Looks like Walter Trinidad. What's left of him is still over at the county dock. The cops are keeping everyone back now that they finally got here, but I can tell you, I got a good look, and it ain't a pretty sight. You can see right off he was murdered."

"Murdered? How can you tell that?" I asked, my curiosity getting the better of me.

"Well, for one thing, there's still a bit of rope tied around one ankle bone. Apparently somebody tried to weigh him down with something. And, well, you're not going to believe this, but there's something missing that I doubt seriously is on account of the fish." When I arched my eyebrows indicating more than mild interest, Jess cut his engine and leaned out the window, speaking in a near-whisper. "Now I'm not making this up, Cassidy. It looks like somebody done whacked off the bastard's pecker."

"What?" I asked incredulously. "How can you be sure that it, uh, wasn't part of the, uh . . . well, that the fish didn't do it?"

Jess reached into his pocket and pulled out a self-rolled cigarette. The first time I'd seen him do this, I'd thought he was lighting up a joint, but in fact he was probably the most frugal man I knew, and rolling his own cigarettes was the only way he could afford to smoke. He took his time lighting it, obviously enjoying my curiosity.

"The thing is, you can tell the parts the fish got, because they sort of nibbled the man to pieces. It's all torn-like where they went after him. Take his face, for example. Ain't nothing left of his cheeks above the beard, and his lips are all but gone. Eyes got munched at pretty good too. But the dick, if you'll pardon my French, is not like that at all. It's sliced clean off like it was done with a butcher knife. Now the balls, they were nibbled at plenty."

I could tell Jess was enjoying himself enormously, but I was getting a tad queasy. "Uh, okay, Jess. I get the picture. By the way, did you happen to notice if one of the cops on the scene was Martha?"

Jess had met Martha on a few occasions while doing odd jobs around the house, and the three of us had gotten good and drunk one afternoon when a storm had come up and we were all forced inside to wait it out. The two of them had gotten on famously.

"She sure is. That's why I've been driving all over town trying to track you down. It seems she's gotten you a client."

Jess was one of the few locals who knew about my new vocation, and he was tickled pink with the image of me as a private eye.

"What do you mean, she got me a client?" I asked, suddenly panic-stricken.

"Well, that's what she said. She asked me if I could find you on account of she'd got you a client and you better hurry on over to the dock or she'll be gone."

"Who's the client?" I asked.

He shrugged. "She was spending an awful lot of time talking to some woman. A real looker, too. So I figure that's who it is, but she didn't tell me any more than that. You want a ride?"

Jess's truck had the smell that afflicted so many of the houses on the lake — mildew and rain rot — but I'd walked enough for one day, so I climbed in.

The police had cordoned off the entire east dock and the onlookers were forced to stand up on park tables to get a glimpse of the corpse being lifted onto a gurney and slid into the back of a Kings Harbor ambulance. I was glad I'd been spared a first-hand look at Walter Trinidad's body, Jess's description having been enough to last me quite a while. I scanned the clusters of police officers who were mostly standing around talking and spotted Martha talking to a young woman. She was, as Jess put it, a looker. Martha was no slouch herself, when it came to looks. While she constantly lamented her tendency to gain weight, in truth, most of it was distributed in well-defined muscle. With her big, brown eyes and dimpled cheeks, she would be considered attractive by most people, but the woman she was talking to was stunning. She had black hair, cut fashionably short, which accentuated her chiseled cheekbones and wide-set eyes. She was dressed casually in slacks and an oversized sweater which did little to conceal the fashion-model's body beneath. As I approached, I was suddenly conscious of still being dressed in sweats and tennis shoes. Martha glanced up and waved me over enthusiastically.

"Cass, I'm glad you're here," she said. "This is Erica Trinidad. Erica, this is Cassidy James, the private investigator I told you about."

"Pleased to meet you. " She shook my hand with a firm, even grip.

"The pleasure is all mine," I said, feeling like an absolute idiot. No one actually says "The pleasure is all mine." Where I had dredged this up, I had no idea, but those startling blue eyes had me tongue-tied.

"Erica," Martha went on, "is the niece of the recently deceased. She's been visiting for a few days on her way up North and finds herself in the unenviable position of being the only kin in the area. For the time being, we've asked her to stay in town and she's agreed, but she's anxious to get on her way

14

and asked me if I knew of anyone in the private sector who might expedite the investigation. Naturally, I thought of you."

Martha was practically drooling over this woman, using up all the big words she knew, and I hated to disappoint her, but I had no intention of getting involved in something this far over my head.

"I'm sorry, Ms. Trinidad," I said. "But I'm afraid my friend here has overstated my qualifications. I have no experience with murder cases, and if in fact that's what this turns out to be, I doubt I could be of much help. I'm sure the police will do everything they can to handle the situation expeditiously." I smiled sweetly at Martha, thinking "Touche!"

"Oh, it was murder all right," Erica said. "I'm not even surprised it happened. My uncle, I'm sorry to say, was a loathsome pig. And a lech to boot. But right now the police are treating me as if I'm a suspect, and frankly I'm not real comfortable leaving this in the hands of that Sergeant Grimes. He seems a little gruff."

"Sergeant Grimes?" I asked Martha. Sergeant Grimes had been Martha's personal nemesis in the KHPD for years. He was famous for his good ol' boy attitude, and Martha definitely did not fit his idea of a model officer, not to mention that of a lady. She'd heard he regularly called her "Butchie" behind her back. Once she'd called him on it, saying she didn't appreciate the unprofessional nickname, to which he artfully replied, "Hey, if the foo shits, wear it."

"Yeah, Grimes is all hot to trot on this, so I'm sure he'll do a bang-up job, but still, Cass, it couldn't hurt to have someone else do some tactful nosing about." She smiled at Erica. "Cass here is a top-notch detective who might just be able to bring a different perspective to the case."

I shot Martha a withering look, but she was beaming at Erica and didn't seem to notice.

Erica said, "Well, I'd be extremely grateful to have you look into it, Ms. James." Her voice was deep and sexy like Suzanne Pleshette's, and I found myself grinning at her like a fool.

"Cassidy's fine," I said. "Or Cass. I'm not much into formalities."

"Cass, then," she said. "The thing is, I just didn't have a good feeling about Sergeant Grimes and, well, as much as I didn't particularly like my Uncle Walter, I still feel somewhat obligated to help find his murderer. You will help me on this, won't you? I mean, if it's a question of money, well, that's not a problem. By the way, what is your fee?"

Before I could stop myself, I blurted out the amount that my mentor, Jake Parcell, had charged for his services, fifty dollars an hour, plus expenses. The next thing I knew, we were shaking on it, and I had my first, honest-to-God client.

Chapter Three

While the police were still sorting things out, I offered Erica a ride back to her uncle's place in my boat, hoping she could shed some light on the case. We rode in silence until we reached Walter Trinidad's house, which sat far back on a heavily forested acre with six hundred feet of lake frontage. The hedges were all immaculately trimmed into fish and bird shapes, reminding me of Disneyland. Both of his boats, an aluminum Boston Whaler bass-fishing boat, and an iridescent turquoise speedboat, were securely moored in the boathouse next to his dock. I hopped out of my Sea Swirl and tied up to the dock while Erica deftly took care of the bow line.

"Looks like you know your way around boats." I peered into Trinidad's boats. Both were in immaculate shape, as if he'd recently washed and waxed them. My own boat was in need of some TLC, and I admired the highly polished sheen of his speedboat. Running my hand along the smooth surface, I noticed a cigarette ash on the running board and flicked it into the water.

"I've done some sailing," Erica said. "Mostly in the bay. I'm not much into speedboats. My uncle's idea of boating was to make as much noise and wake as possible. It used to drive me crazy when I was a kid."

"Can I ask you something personal?" I asked, turning to face her. "It's obvious you didn't care much for your uncle. Why were you visiting him in the first place?"

Erica smiled, exposing straight, white teeth and little crinkly lines at the corners of her eyes, but her smile seemed sad. "Uncle Walter was my father's brother. My father died when I was ten, and every year my aunt and uncle invited me up here for the summer, to give my mom a break, I guess. Aunt Penny was okay, a little mousy, but Uncle Walter has always given me the creeps. He used to pat me, you know? Nothing overtly sexual, but just inappropriate. He'd wink at me, like we shared some secret, and he always insisted on kissing me hello and good-bye on the lips. Anyway, I quit coming up here when I turned sixteen, and except for one Thanksgiving, I haven't seen him since. My Aunt Penny finally divorced him this past year and moved to Florida.

The first smart thing she ever did. His own kids, my cousins, never could stand him, and from what I understand, they haven't seen him in ages. Anyway, the only reason I decided to stop on my way up to Canada was to deliver something to him. Come on, I'll show you."

Erica led the way up a meandering brick path between the fish- and bird-shaped hedges to the front door. Like most of the houses on the lake, the door was unlocked, and we walked right into the spacious wood- and glass-lined living room.

"Here," she said, gesturing. "He never even got the chance to hang it."

Leaning against the wall was a portrait of two young boys and a pony. The smaller of the boys had dark hair and wide-set, piercing blue eyes and looked strikingly like Erica herself. He sat atop the pony, while the bigger boy held the reins.

"My father and uncle. My mom had it hanging in her living room for years, but she's moved into a smaller apartment now, and there's no room for it. The only person I could think of who might want it was Uncle Walter, and since I was coming this way, I decided to deliver it in person. Besides, I've always loved this place. It was just him I didn't like. But now I feel guilty saying that. Anyway, that's why I'm here."

We moved into the kitchen where Erica went about making tea while I scrounged around for paper and a pen I could use to jot down notes.

"I need to know everything he did from the minute you arrived, even things that might not seem important," I said. "I know you've already been questioned by the police this morning, and if you'd rather do this later, we can, but the sooner I can get started, the better chance we'll have of making progress."

Erica set a plate of what looked like zucchini bread between us and sat down across from me. "I had nothing else to do yesterday, so I baked," she explained. "Go ahead, ask away."

"When exactly did you get here?"

"The day before yesterday. Wednesday about three. I called ahead from Eureka to let him know I was coming. He seemed genuinely pleased. I told him I had something for him and he insisted I spend the night. Despite everything, I figured I could take care of myself, so I agreed. He met me at the marina about three and asked if I'd mind waiting while he ran into McGregors for a few things. I told him I'd join him, just to stretch my legs, and we walked over."

"How did he greet you?" I asked.

"You mean did he kiss me on the lips? Some things never change. But I've grown up now. I turned my cheek at the last second." She smiled and took a bite of zucchini bread. I followed suit. It was delicious.

"Anyway, I could tell he was the same old Uncle Walter, bossing around the grocery clerk and berating the bag boy for having put something heavy on top of the bread the last time he'd been in. I was embarrassed to be seen with him, to be honest, and I pretended not to know him." She paused, a brief smile crossing her face. "After that, we went back to the marina, and it took forever because Uncle Walter kept stopping to talk to people. It was weird, like he was showing me off, except he didn't tell anyone I

20

was his niece. I got the feeling he wanted people to think I was his girlfriend."

"Who did he stop and talk to?" I asked.

"I didn't really know any of them. One was the woman who runs Loggers Tavern. She was out sweeping the sidewalk in front of the bar, and my uncle shouted something like, 'Hey Lizzie, you got any decent wine in yet?' What was she supposed to say? 'No, Walter, just the same old rotgut as yesterday!'? He didn't talk with anyone for very long, it was like he just wanted to impress me that he knew everyone." She paused and added thoughtfully, "Or impress them that he had a woman with him. The thing is, the more he tried to impress me, the less he did. And I didn't get the feeling he was impressing anyone else either."

"Who else did he talk to?" I asked, helping myself to more bread and sipping the tea she'd placed before me.

"Well, the marina owner, Gus, was out working on a truck, and my uncle yelled over to him. Something about when was he going to finish putting on the new dock bumpers, that he was tired of scraping up his boat."

This made perfect sense, since I, too, was a little peeved at the missing bumpers. Anything short of a perfect docking resulted in scratches on the hull, and with the tide fluctuations of the creek, which ran from the lake to the ocean, perfect dockings were rare. I'd even asked Gus myself when the new bumpers were coming in, but I imagined Walter Trinidad had been less than tactful.

"Gus said the bumpers were on order and my uncle stomped away like he was really ticked off.

Then Gus muttered something like 'If you'd learn to handle a boat, you damned cowboy, you wouldn't have no scratches.' "

"Cowboy" was the term Gus Townsend bestowed upon all Californians, though I was never quite sure why. I wondered if behind my back he referred to me as a cowgirl. To my face, he'd always been polite enough, but you never knew.

"The only other person we saw was Tommy, the kid at the marina who helped me put my overnight bag and the portrait on the boat. He seemed real nice, but he smelled terrible. A little deodorant would have gone a long way. Anyway, Uncle Walter was even rude to him, calling him 'Tinkerbell' when he tripped on the dock. Like I said, I'm not surprised someone would want to murder him. He turned out to be even more disagreeable than I'd remembered."

I was writing as fast as I could, trying to keep up with Erica's fast-paced account. I found it was easier to concentrate if I didn't look directly into her eyes. "What happened then?" I asked.

"Well, he roared out of the marina going much faster than you're supposed to go through that channel, and I was positive the lake sheriff would stop us, but no one did. I was absolutely dreading my decision to spend the night because I found his company unbearable. As it turned out, though, I didn't have to put up with him for long. We got to the house and by the time he'd fixed himself a drink, the phone rang and shortly after that he left again."

"Any idea who called?" I asked.

"None at all. I didn't hear any of the conversation because I was in the bathroom, and when I came out, he said he had to run somewhere for a minute, to make myself at home and when he got back, we'd hang the portrait. He even opened a bottle of decent Chardonnay for me before he left, which for him was a pretty classy gesture. It was the last I saw of him."

"What did you do?" I asked.

"Well, mostly I sat around and drank wine. I mean, at first it was really relaxing, and I was glad he was gone so I could unwind from the long drive. I sat out on the front deck for a while, looking at the lake, but it got cold, so I went back in. I made a fire when it got dark and eventually I made myself some dinner. I kept thinking he'd come back with steaks or something, so I held off, but by nine I was starving, so I heated a can of soup. I called the marina, to see if his boat was there, but no one answered. I called the Cedar Hills Lodge and got the numbers for all the bars in town. I figured he was probably at one of them, but he wasn't. I didn't know any of his friends. In fact, I'm not sure he had any. Finally I made up a bed in one of the guest rooms and went to sleep. It's funny, because I thought he came home sometime in the middle of the night, but maybe I dreamed it."

"What do you mean?" I asked, my curiosity piqued.

"Well, I can't be sure, but I thought I heard him bumping into things in his room, and I figured he was probably drunk. I remember being glad I had locked the door, but then I fell back to sleep, and I dreamed about the same thing, so in the morning I wasn't sure if I had dreamed the whole thing or if I had actually heard him. I guess all that wine didn't help. Anyway, when I got up, I tiptoed past his room so I wouldn't wake him, but his door was wide open and the bed was made. I decided I must have dreamed the whole thing, but now that he's been found dead, it makes me wonder if maybe someone had actually been there while I was sleeping."

I put my pen down and got up to stretch. Being in such close proximity to this woman was beginning to agitate me. I wasn't sure why, but she had a disturbing effect on my equilibrium. "From the time you arrived on Wednesday, until yesterday morning when you reported him missing, you must have had time to look around. Did you notice anything different or missing?"

"Not that I could tell, but then I didn't exactly inventory his belongings. I didn't go into his room at all until I knew he was missing. I was hoping to find an address book, or list of friends' phone numbers or something, but I struck out. Finally, I called the Kings Harbor Police Department and tried to file a missing persons report, but it hadn't been twenty-four hours yet. I checked the local hospitals, but of course he wasn't there. Gus said his car was still parked at the marina, too. That's when I went down to the dock and noticed both boats were in the boat-house, so either he had come back in the night, or someone else had brought his boat back for him, because I had definitely seen him leave in his speed-boat Wednesday night. I did everything I could think of yesterday, and was getting ready to call the police again this morning when someone called from the county dock to tell me my uncle was dead and did I want them to come pick me up so I could give the police a positive ID."

For the first time since she had begun talking, I

could see the strain she must have been under. Her striking blue eyes looked tired, and her account had been punctuated by sighs, a sure sign of stress. I decided to leave her alone for a while so she could get some rest and make the inevitable arrangements and family phone calls. I also knew it wouldn't be long before the house would be descended upon by Kings Harbor's finest. Already, as I looked out toward the lake, I could see the unmistakable orange and white of the sheriff's boat rounding Cedar Point.

"Erica," I said, putting my notes in order. "I'm afraid you're in for a long day. From the looks of it, the sheriff is heading this way, and my guess is that Sergeant Grimes is either with him or close behind. They'll be all over this place and probably make you go through the whole story again."

She stood looking out the window at the approaching boat, and a flash of panic clouded her face. "God, what if they really do consider me a suspect?" she said. "I mean, how can I prove I didn't kill him? It's not like I have an alibi!"

I walked over and took both her hands, turning her to face me. I wasn't at all prepared for the feelings that surged through me when I looked into her eyes, and I did my best to ignore the pounding in my heart.

"Listen," I said. "First of all, you can't start doubting yourself. Just be honest with them. Be helpful. Tell them everything. If it looks like they do consider you a valid suspect, call me immediately. I know a lawyer in Kings Harbor who can help you. If you need to get away from here, I've got room at my place, which is just the other side of Blue Heron Bay.

You're welcome to crash there, make phone calls, whatever you need. I can understand your not wanting to stay here any longer than necessary."

For a minute, I thought she was going to cry. Her eyes misted over and she smiled the way I do when I'm embarrassed at my own emotions. "You really are too kind," she said. "And I may just take you up on your offer."

"Well don't even hesitate. For now, I'm going to do a little nosing around, but my answering machine is on, and I won't be far away." I gathered up my notes, leaving my phone number and directions to my house on the table.

"I can't thank you enough," she said, following me to the door.

"I haven't done anything yet," I answered. "Just keep your fingers crossed. Maybe this thing will be over as quickly as it started."

She crossed her fingers and waved them at me as I walked down to the dock, where the Cedar Hills Sheriff, two uniformed officers and Sergeant Grimes were tying up behind my boat.

"Good morning," I said to Sheriff Tom Booker, who eyed me curiously.

With his thick white hair and dark tanned face, he was as handsome as ever, but his usual cheerfulness was gone. "Cassidy James. What brings you out to the Trinidad place this morning?"

Surely he didn't think *I* had snuffed the poor lecherous bastard! "Well actually, I'm on a case."

"A what?" He peered at me from the boat while the others scrambled awkwardly onto the dock. It was obvious none of them was accustomed to life on the water. I reached into my boat where I actually had some brand new business cards stashed in a side pocket and handed one to the sheriff.

"Erica Trinidad has hired me to find out who killed her uncle," I said, thinking I sounded somewhat absurd.

"That's absurd!" the fat Sergeant Grimes barked from behind me, confirming my suspicion. It was clear, no one was going to take me seriously as a private eye. But that was their problem.

"Don't you think this is a job better suited to the police?" Sheriff Booker asked, not unkindly. "And since when are you a private investigator anyway?"

I wished I'd brought my license with me so I could flash it at him, but I hadn't come prepared for detective work that morning.

"Yes, I do think this is a job for the police," I said somewhat testily. "I have no intention of impeding your investigation in any way, and I'm happy to share whatever I find with you, in the spirit of collaboration."

"We don't need no effing collaboration, missy," Sergeant Grimes growled. "Just be damn sure you stay outta the way. You so much as touch one piece of evidence, mess up our investigation in any way, and I'll haul your ass in for interfering with police business."

"Don't tell me," I said, losing my resolve to remain polite, "you must be Sergeant Grimes."

"That's right. What of it?"

"Your reputation for charm precedes you," I managed, straight faced. "Good day, gentlemen." With that, I finished untying my bowline and hopped into my pretty, blue boat. I couldn't help noticing the amusement in the other officers' eyes. Grimes himself was red-faced and seething.

Sheriff Booker grabbed onto the side of my boat and said in a low voice, "Cassie, you best stay out of Grimes's way. He's got jurisdiction on this, and he takes that kind of stuff seriously. Since it happened on the lake, I've got some pull, but the bottom line is, it's his baby. And for God's sake, be careful," he added. "Whoever did this, well, they weren't messing around."

"Thank you, Sheriff. I appreciate the advice. I'll be just as careful as I can." I eased the throttle into forward, pulling away from the dock.

Chapter Four

I headed back to my place, mulling over the morning's events. A couple of things bothered me, and I wanted to sort out my thoughts before I drew up any kind of action plan. For one ·thing, I didn't like the fact that Trinidad's boat was back in his boathouse. How had it gotten there and when? I also didn't like the fact that his penis had been cut off, although the police had not yet made that official. I supposed Trinidad hadn't liked that part much either. Cutting off someone's privates, I thought, tended to be a very personal kind of thing and reeked of some warped sense of revenge. That meant someone had to be extremely ticked off at him. I doubted even Trinidad could make the average Joe that mad. And where was the missing penis, anyway? Had someone whacked it off in a fit of rage à la Lorena Bobbitt? No doubt Sergeant Grimes would be pursuing that angle, with Erica Trinidad as his prime suspect. Which of course wasn't completely out of the realm of possibility. It's true she'd hired me to find the killer, but perhaps that was a ploy on her part to convince us of her innocence. But somehow I didn't think both Martha's and my instincts could be that far off. And it seemed to me, if she had killed her uncle, she was smart enough to have constructed an alibi for herself. There was something else niggling at the back of my mind that I couldn't quite put my finger on. Something that might be important, but no matter how hard I tried to bring it into focus, it danced away like a shadow on a wall.

Panic and Gammon greeted me vociferously at the front door, as they always did, butting their heads against me as I tried to enter without letting them out.

Half Bengal and half Egyptian Mau, they were a stunning pair. Where tabbies had stripes, these two had spots, but their coloring was as different as their size. Panic, as lithe and agile as her Bengal father, had black spots on a silky, silver background. Her tail was incredibly long, as were her legs. Her eyes, the color of gooseberries, matched her sister's, but weren't as large, or as beautiful.

The bigger sister, Gammon, was a striking beauty and terribly fat. She had rich brown spots on a silver, cream and caramel background. Her fur was so plush you could lose your fingers in it. Somehow, little Panic had gotten her sister's share of tail, and poor, fat Gammon had an embarrassingly short, thick one. When she ran, her belly swayed back and forth, which never failed to make me laugh. It was hard to say which cat was my favorite — beautiful, fat Gammon with her intelligent, green eyes that made me wonder what she spent so much time thinking about, or the skittish, playful huntress Panic, who feared no other animal but leaped a foot at the sound of twigs rustling in the breeze.

They had been Martha's house-warming gift three years earlier, two tiny balls of silky fur no bigger than my palm. Somehow she had known that it would take more than just one cat to fill the void left by Diane. And while not even a dozen cats could have done that, these two had turned into loving, wonderful companions.

"Come on you little rug rats," I said, hefting fat Gammon up and hoisting her onto my shoulder. "Let's see what we can scrounge up for lunch."

After opening a can of Gourmet Kitty which they politely shared, I fixed myself a ham and Swiss on rye with mayo and mustard, with a dill pickle for good measure, and sat down at the kitchen table to organize my thoughts. I was deep into my reverie, when the annoying whine of a speedboat buzzed my dock. Looking out, I could see Jess Martin's son, Dougie, at the wheel of a bright red Jet Boat. The boat was full of laughing boys, some of whom I recognized from town. Their bare chests were tanned from the summer sun, and they laughed as they threw a wake onto my dock. While I knew Jess would get after Dougie if he saw him driving his boat this way, for a moment I envied the boys and their carefree summertime mischief. I watched them do a three-sixty in front of my neighbor's dock, sending a spray of water into his moored dinghy, and then they raced off across the lake, leaving giant waves in their wake that rocked my boat violently against the dock. Unable to concentrate any further, I decided it was time to change and get busy with my investigation.

Chapter Five

While the Cedar Hills Lodge was the preferred
watering hole for tourists, most of the locals I wanted
to talk to would be at Loggers Tavern. By five
o'clock the place was nearly packed, and there was
an undeniable touch of festivity in the air. It seemed
the death of Walter Trinidad had cheered a good
many souls in Cedar Hills.

"Well, look what the cat drug in," I heard a
familiar voice shout as I entered. I peered through
the dimly lit, smoke-filled room and made out the
hazy but unmistakably tall outline of my friend Jess

33

Martin, who waved me over to a stool next to him at the bar. "I thought you was hot on the trail of the Cedar Hills Killer," he teased as I plunked myself onto the stool. I'd noticed that whenever Jess was around other locals, his Cedar Hills accent tended to increase tenfold. Laughter rippled around the horseshoe-shaped bar, and as my eyes adjusted to the dim interior, I made out the faces of Buddy Drake, the mail carrier who'd found the body, and Gus Townsend, the marina owner.

"I see you boys have been celebrating," I said, settling into my own adaptation of the Cedar Hills drawl. I didn't really do this intentionally, but for some reason, whenever I was in the company of two or more locals, I found myself mimicking their peculiar accents. I'd tried to stop myself from doing this at first, but of late I'd sort of given in to it. It seemed to be an irresistible urge.

"Buy this good-lookin' lady a drink!" Gus shouted to Lizzie, the bartender, in his usual raspy voice. His craggy, weather-worn face made him appear much older than his fifty some-odd years. "She's gonna track down the man who done snipped off Walter Trinidad's pinky," he croaked, a wicked grin cracking his leathery face. This brought on a whole slew of guffaws from around the bar.

"Yeah." Buddy was sitting on my left. "And when she do, we gonna give the sonofabitch a medal!" The laughter that followed was accompanied by palms slapping the bar and a whole array of hoots and hollers. Obviously these fellows weren't recent arrivals at the tavern. By the general ruddiness of their cheeks and the gleam in their eyes, I'd say that most of them had been there since lunch, which I assumed had been of a primarily liquid nature.

Lizzie Thompson set a pint of draft beer in front of me and cracked a toothy grin. "Is it true, Cass? You really a private detective like Jess here says?" Her husky voice spoke of too many nights keeping up with the boys in booze and cigarettes. She winked at me, and not for the first time I wondered if Lizzie Thompson wouldn't be happier running a women's bar.

"That's right, Lizzie. I am. And not that I wouldn't normally just drop in to enjoy the company, but truth is, I was hoping someone here might be able to give me a hand."

"What do you need, Cass?" Jess asked, sliding his empty mug toward Lizzie, who promptly refilled it.

"Well, first off, I'm trying to figure out when was the last time someone actually saw Walter Trinidad alive."

"I seen him late Wednesday afternoon, struttin' around the marina with some out-of-town broad," Gus said. "He was bitchin' and cryin' about the fact he couldn't park his boat right without scratching his precious paint job."

"I saw him too." Lizzie's dark eyes were shining. "Came by the bar to criticize my wine selection. I didn't pay him a lick of attention, but I did notice the girl. Way outta his league, if you ask me."

Buddy Drake cleared his throat, and the whole bar quieted. Since having found the body, it seemed Buddy had acquired a certain hero's status. He tugged on his scraggly black moustache and sat up straighter on his bar stool. He was in his forties and his coal-black hair was beginning to thin, a fact nearly concealed by his ever-present baseball cap. Not much over five feet tall, Buddy still carried himself with a distinct air of confidence, and despite his short stature, most folks in Cedar Hills seemed to look up to him as a leader.

"The way I figure," he said, pausing for effect, "the girl's your best bet, Cass. Usually, when a guy gets his dinger bobbed, it's what you call a crime of passion."

Apparently Buddy Drake had also become an expert on the psychological profile of the murdering mind.

"But I hear the girl's still here, holed up at Trinidad's place this whole time," Jess said. "If I was her, and I'd killed someone, I'd have hightailed it out of here long before now."

"Well, Sheriff Booker told *me* the girl in question was the niece," Lizzie said. "I don't see how a blood relation is apt to do to an uncle what was done to Walter Trinidad."

"He didn't seem to be treating her in no uncleish fashion that I could see," Gus said, downing what looked like straight bourbon.

"Maybe he tried to get a little too friendly and the lady just freaked," said Buddy. The others nodded.

"Is that who hired you?" Jess asked. "The guy's niece?"

"Actually, Jess, that's confidential information." I knew that this would automatically confirm it. The last thing Erica needed was the whole town thinking she'd killed her uncle. Maybe if they knew she'd hired someone to find the killer, they'd be less inclined to suspect her. On the other hand, maybe that's why she did hire me, to throw people off. I pictured her face, those intelligent, blue eyes, and wondered if I could be that wrong about her character. "Did anyone see Walter Trinidad after he left the marina? Anyone call him, or hear of someone else calling him?"

General silence filled the smoky room, and as if on cue, most of the men reached for their cigarettes. The rest of the nation may have heard that smoking was hazardous to the health, but the news had apparently not yet reached Cedar Hills.

Since my query had received no answer, I tried another tack.

"If someone had called him, who would it be? I mean, he must have had *some* friends in town."

"Not that I ever saw," Jess said.

"Weren't nobody could stand him much," added Gus. "Only reason I even let him have a slip at the marina is 'cause I charge him price and a half and he was too damn arrogant to complain about it. Now I gotta find some other cowboy to fill the slip."

The others chuckled, but the mood was beginning to turn from boisterous to nasty. I imagined Gus Townsend was not a pleasant drunk, and having seen him at the marina on many a morning sporting a hangover, I knew that his night of drinking was far from over.

"Well, I sure appreciate you fellows helping out and all." I downed the last of my beer. "If you all hear of anything that might help, just call me. I'd sure like to know who Trinidad was planning to meet that night."

This perked up their interest.

"How do you know he was?" Buddy asked, fingering the bill of his baseball cap.

"Because his niece says he got a call and then left to meet someone."

"She says! Huh! Sounds like she's saving her own hide to me," Gus said.

"The only one I know of who ever called the guy was a bunch of school kids," Jess said. "They used to call him up and say stuff like, 'Hey, Mr. Trinidad, is your refrigerator running? Then you better go catch it!' "

This brought on general laughter and I decided it was a fitting time to depart.

"Well, thanks anyway, guys, and thanks for the beer, Lizzie."

Lizzie's large hands had begun to fidget, and her eyes kept darting toward the little window that looked out onto Main Street. I shot her a questioning look, but she snapped back into focus and just like that, whatever had been bothering her was gone.

"Hell, that's okay, Cass. I put it on Walter Trinidad's bar tab," she said, her gravelly voice full of laughter. "The man once paid a hundred dollars up front to run a tab, but he never came back in after that first time. Said the smoke bothered him too much, and that I had a lousy wine selection. But he never asked for his money back. I figure he wanted folks to think he was so rich, a hundred dollars was pocket change. So tonight, the drinks are on Walter. How about another round, boys?" Glasses were shoved forward and, for the moment at least, it seemed the general good cheer had returned as I eased my way out, into the brightness of what remained of the day.

By six-thirty, I'd talked to everyone I could find who ever knew Walter Trinidad, and the story was the same everywhere. No one knew anything. No one knew anyone else who might know anything. And most of all, no one was surprised or saddened that someone had done him in. There was a lot of head shaking, but no tears were shed. In general, there seemed to be a shared sense that someone, whoever it was, had done the world a favor by speeding Walter Trinidad into the next life.

I was still in the mood for an artichoke and a good steak, so I walked down to McGregors, then decided to call my answering machine from the pay phone outside. I had two messages. One was from Martha, asking me if I'd solved the case yet. Her laughter held the warmth that always put me in a good mood. "Call me, Sherlock, when you get a chance. I've got some news that may interest you. Oh, and give my regards to the lovely Ms. Trinidad." Again, that deep, rich laughter, and then the dial tone. The second call was from Ms. Trinidad herself, asking me to call her as soon as possible. I dug out another twenty cents, and she picked up on the first ring.

"Oh. I'm glad you called, Cass. I was hoping that was you and not another crank call."

"What kind of crank call?" I asked.

"I'll tell you later. Listen. If you don't have dinner plans, how'd you like to join me here? I'm still waiting for a call from my cousin, or I'd get out of here. Can you come over?"

"Sure," I said, my pulse quickening unreasonably. "I was just going to pick up a steak and artichoke at McGregors. If that sounds good, I'll get two."

"That sounds like the nicest offer I've had all day."

By the time I pulled up to Walter Trinidad's dock for the second time that day, the sun was just beginning to disappear over the ridge of giant cedars that lined the west bank of the lake. In the summer, the sky would stay light until almost nine, and dusk was one of my favorite times of day. Erica met me halfway up the walk and took one of the bags out of my hands. The fading light played upon her dark skin, and I noted for the third or fourth time that day that she was truly an attractive woman.

"This looks like more than two steaks," she said, peering into one bag.

"Well, I didn't know your status on charcoal and wine, and I thought we might as well make a salad. I hope you like blue cheese and raspberry vinaigrette. Oh, and I found a portobello mushroom we can sauté in olive oil." I followed her into the house where she had already drawn the blinds on all the windows. "Tell me about the crank call," I said, finding a corkscrew in the first drawer I checked.

As I opened a bottle of Napa Cabernet, Erica began to trim the artichokes. It was strange, I thought. I barely knew this woman, and yet we were working side by side in the kitchen like two old friends. There was a calmness about her that made me instantly at ease. At the same time, every time our eyes met, I felt a distinct fluttering in my chest. It had been so long since I felt like this that I wasn't sure I should trust the feeling, so I did my best to avoid looking at her at all.

"I've had two calls, actually," she said. "The first one came about five o'clock. I answered the phone and someone started going 'Glub, glub. Glub, glub, glub.' Like the sound something makes when it's going under water."

"Charming," I said. "And the second call?"

"It came right before you called. About seven. This time they talked in a falsetto. I couldn't even tell if it was a man or a woman. Whoever it was said 'Say good night, Walter. Good night, Walter!' and then there was this sick laughter and they hung up."

I handed Erica a glass of wine and took a long swallow myself. "Have you told the police yet? Maybe they can put a tap on your line, in case you get more calls."

"I was hoping you could call your friend Martha. I really can't stand that Sergeant Grimes, even if he is in charge of the investigation. The Sheriff was okay, though. Maybe we should call him?"

"Well, we should definitely tell someone. This person sounds pretty warped. Any idea how old they were?"

"I have no idea. The first time they were singing, and even that was done in a kind of falsetto. Obviously, he or she was trying to disguise their voice."

"Let me get the coals started, and then I'll give Martha a call. By the way, she said to give you her regards."

Erica blushed. Very interesting, I thought as I took the charcoal to the back deck. Martha might be able to tell a lesbian a mile away, but I was still

41

having trouble figuring Erica out. She certainly didn't dress like so many dykes I knew, in Levi's and a flannel shirt. Tonight she was sporting a navy blue silk blouse hanging loosely over white chinos. Simple, but classy. She had the self-assurance and assertiveness that seemed the hallmark of so many lesbians, even during what was obviously a trying ordeal, and I had to admit, my instincts told me she was probably gay. On the other hand, she'd done nothing to indicate an interest in either men *or* women, and I had no reason to assume that she was anything but straight. Still, there was that unmistakable blush at the mention of Martha's interest.

It was just her luck, I thought, to instantly snag the best-looking woman to hit the Oregon Coast in three years. Not that I would have been interested, I told myself, but it *was* rather amusing. Having been celibate for almost three years, I wasn't at all sure I'd know what to do even if I were interested. Which I definitely wasn't, I told myself again, ignoring the fluttering in my stomach. I dialed Martha's number and told her about the calls.

"I can probably get a tap put on her line by tomorrow, in case she gets another one, and we should be able to trace the calls she got today. Listen, Cass, I think she'd be better off at the Cedar Hills Lodge. This guy sounds like a real head case. And it looks like what everyone thought was right on. The victim's penis *was* sliced off, not just eaten away by the fish like the rest of him. It seems Grimes is half convinced that Erica's the perp. He needs to know about these calls. The sooner you can get him off her back, the sooner he'll start looking for someone else. But I know this guy, Cass. He's a bulldog. Once he gets an idea in his fat head, he can't let it go."

"I think I'll call Sheriff Booker," I said. "He might listen to me, and I think Grimes might listen to him. Unfortunately, I doubt your friend Grimes would listen to one thing I had to say to him. I'm afraid I've already ticked him off."

"That figures. The guy's not just homophobic, he's woman-phobic! Not to change the subject, but how's Grimes's number one suspect holding up?"

"Pretty well, considering," I said. "I think between being grilled by cops all day and getting those phone calls, she's a little gun shy. As soon as we finish dinner, I'm going to ask her over to my place. I agree with you, staying here is not a good idea."

"Oh ho!" Martha said. "I see."

"What?" I asked. "You see what?" The silence that followed answered my question perfectly. At that moment, Erica walked back into the room and I was unable to defend myself at all. Well, I'd set Martha straight later. In the meantime, her chuckling was making my face turn hot. "Listen, I've got to go," I said. "I want to talk to Sheriff Booker before it gets too late. Let me know what you find out about the phone tap, okay?"

"Sure thing, lover," she said, laughing. "And take care of yourself. I'll talk to you tomorrow." I hung up, trying not to be irked by Martha's devious, one-track mind.

I reached Sheriff Booker on my first try and explained about the two crank calls. I then told him I might be taking Ms. Trinidad to my place for the night and left my number. Unlike Martha, he didn't see anything untoward in this, in fact complimenting me on the prudence of this decision.

"And keep an eye on her, Cass. I don't rightly know what to think of this murder yet. My gut tells me that that little lady didn't have a thing to do with any of it. But my gut hasn't always been right, either. For now, she's about the only suspect anyone's got, so for God's sake, don't let her slip away on you. If she is innocent, and she's been getting these calls like she says, then she may be in some kind of danger herself. Your idea of getting her out of that house is a good one. By the way," he said, "you come across anything of interest today?"

"Only what I already suspected," I said, "which was that if hating a man is motive for murder, then just about everyone in Cedar Hills had a motive."

"Me included," he said, chuckling. "I never could stand that arrogant S.O.B."

By the time I got through making calls, Erica had set the table, prepared a salad, put the steaks on the grill and poured us each another glass of wine. The daylight had finally faded into night and I knew that soon the tiny bats that inhabit the woodlands would be unfolding their ungainly wings to swoop down upon the lake for their evening feast of mosquitos and moths. It was usually at this time of night I made a point of heading indoors.

We brought the steaks in and bustled about getting everything we needed for our own feast. By now, Erica admitted, she was ravenous, having not eaten a thing since the zucchini bread that morning.

I lied and said I hadn't eaten anything since then either. We dug into the meal with equal vigor, and our conversation moved easily, without the awkwardness that usually accompanies first meals. It was funny, I mused, how a crisis could bind complete strangers together so quickly. When the meal was nearly over, the phone rang, and I jumped to get it, my heart pounding at the prospect of hearing the crank caller myself. But it was Erica's cousin, finally returning her call, and I cleaned up the kitchen while she finished making arrangements for her uncle's service.

When at last we managed to get things in order, it was well after ten. I had convinced her to bundle up her few belongings for an overnight stay at my house, and we boarded my boat, bringing the last of the wine with us. No point in having a good cabernet go to waste.

The night was clear and calm. Stars studded the inky sky, and a sliver of moon sat way over to the east, shedding a faint light across the water. I turned on my running lights and putt-putted toward Blue Heron Bay. There was no reason to hurry, and I preferred to take it slow at night, not just because it was safer, but because I loved the sounds and smells of the lake at night. And I had to admit, I enjoyed having Erica in the boat beside me.

"Is it always this beautiful?" she asked, looking up at the sky.

"Actually, I don't come out that much after dark. Too many things to look out for, like logs in the water." As soon as I said this, I wished I hadn't. The awkward silence told me Erica too was thinking of the last "log" someone ran into.

"Hey, what's that over there?" she asked, pointing toward the shore of Pebble Cove. I'd seen it the same time she had, the unearthly orange glow of something on fire.

"Better hang on," I said, and thrust the throttle forward, heading for shore. As we neared, the orange flames leapt into sight and I could make out the outline of a two-story house engulfed by flames. The air was already thick with smoke and I could hear voices shouting in front of the house. Heading away from the shore was the barely distinguishable outline of another boat, without running lights. Someone was probably going for help and hadn't turned on the lights yet. It's funny the details you notice when a crisis is at hand and time slows down beyond reason. I remember thinking how odd the boat looked, with little orange dots like fireflies suspended above it, as it moved farther and farther away from the shore.

But time slammed itself back into full speed as I pulled up to the dock. Erica had already leaped out of the boat and was securing the stern line to a metal cleat on the dock. I jumped out and we both raced toward the house. It was lucky, I thought, that the house was in a clearing instead of surrounded by trees. There was no access road to most of the houses on the lake, meaning that no fire truck would be coming to save the day. Any fire fighting would be done by us. With any luck, it would burn itself out before spreading elsewhere.

Standing on the front walkway, clutching each other, were two women in pajamas, obviously mother and daughter. The daughter, about fifteen or sixteen, was sobbing and both were looking up to an upstairs window, in which I could see the outline of a small figure. Just then, a tall, slightly overweight man came bursting out through the front door, gasping and choking.

I ran over and shouted above the roar of the fire, "What can we do to help?"

"My daughter's trapped! I can't get to her! The stairwell's on fire!"

"Do you have a ladder?" I shouted.

"Yes, but it's inside!"

"How about a blanket? Or a tarp?"

He looked at me, clearly panic-stricken.

"Erica!" I yelled. "In the bow of my boat, left-hand side, beneath the seat. I've got a canvas boat cover!" She was already halfway down the path, running at full speed. I rushed to where the mother and daughter were standing. The mother had picked up a garden hose and was aiming a futile spray of water toward the towering flames. "How old is the girl?"

"Nine," the older daughter answered. "Is she going to die?" she wailed. "Please don't let her die!"

"What's her name?" I asked.

"Mollie," they both answered. I waved my arms at the window and shouted at the top of my lungs. "Mollie! Open the window!"

The reply came back surprisingly strong. "I already did! It's open!"

"Okay, good girl, Mollie. Now, I want you to push out the screen. Can you do that?" I yelled.

We could see her fist pummeling the screen, but it held firm.

"Kick it!" her sister screamed.

"No!" I shouted. "Mollie, listen to me. Do you have something you could throw at the screen? Something heavy?"

Her small frame disappeared and in a minute the leg of a chair came crashing through the screen.

"Good! Now hit it again. Push the screen all the way out!"

After several more tries, both the screen and the chair came tumbling to the ground with a clang. Mollie stood gazing down, a triumphant look on her face. Or perhaps it was hysteria.

Erica had come up behind me and was breathing heavily, the canvas boat cover in her arms. The father had also come over, although he was still choking from the smoke.

"Now, listen," I said. "We've got to all take hold of this canvas and hold it tight like a trampoline. Come on. Let's get right under the window."

"But how do you know it'll hold her?" the mother asked, her voice trembling.

"I *don't* know," I said. "But I don't see any alternative. Come on!" We positioned ourselves beneath the window and held the canvas tight between us, waist high. "Mollie! When I count to three, I want you to jump onto this safety net. Do you hear me?"

"Yes," came the reply. I sensed her bravery fading fast.

"You can do this, Mollie." Flames surged through the roof, not more than ten feet from where she stood. If she didn't jump soon, it would be too late. "Okay! On the count of three. One. Two. THREE!"

The little girl stood where she was, staring down at us.

"Jump, Mollie!" I shouted.

"Come on honey, you can do it!" her father called.

"We're right here!" her mother cried.

"Don't be chicken, Mollie! It's not that far!" her sister yelled.

The word *chicken* must have gotten to her, because with no warning she came hurtling out of the window, like a kid doing a cannonball off the high dive. The force with which she hit the canvas knocked us all flat on our rear ends, and for a brief minute we all lay there, stunned. Mollie got up first and scampered over to her mother.

"I did it! I did it!" she cried. The rest of us scrambled to our feet and took turns hugging one another and Mollie. The thunderous crash of the roof collapsing above Mollie's room, however, sent us all scurrying for the safety of the dock.

"I don't know who you ladies are, or where you came from, but I sure want to thank you," the father said in a voice full of emotion. Erica and I introduced ourselves, and in turn learned that the family beside us were the Hendersons from Los Angeles, here on summer vacation. "I built this house myself," Mr. Henderson said, shaking his head in dismay. "Took me four summers of hard labor. Now it's gone."

We stood and watched as the house slowly burned to the ground. By now, other boats were pulling up to the dock, coming to offer help too late. Still, people filled buckets of lake water and walked around dousing hot spots and stomping on embers.

"Any idea how this started?" I asked the Hendersons.

"Haven't a clue," Mr. Henderson answered. "We

49

were already asleep downstairs. My daughter's screaming woke me, and by that time the whole living room was in flames. I tried to get upstairs to the girls' room, but it was too late."

The older girl, Mary, was very pretty, with long, straw-colored hair and pale skin, now smudged with smoke. Her blue eyes widened. "I woke up because I heard noises. I thought we had a burglar outside, and I came downstairs to turn on the outside lights. That's when I screamed, because the whole living room was on fire. Like Dad said, the stairwell just went up like that, and I couldn't get back up to Mollie. I just started screaming and ran outside."

"Did you see any sign of anyone in the area?" I asked, thinking about the boat I'd seen leaving when we arrived.

"No. I was so scared by the fire, I didn't even think of it again until just now," Mary said, her lower lip beginning to tremble.

"What exactly was it that you heard, honey?" her dad asked.

"Like rustling in the hedges. And maybe voices. It woke me up, and I was all groggy. I looked out the window to see who was here, but it was real dark, so I went down to turn on the outside lights and that's when I saw the fire."

I didn't like the idea that someone had been there just before the fire, and had left quietly in the dark, without running lights. "Can you think of anyone who might want to do this to you?"

"You think somebody did this to us intentionally?" Mrs. Henderson asked, her voice rising. "But why? We don't have any enemies. We hardly know anyone at all up here."

I had no answers, but plenty of questions began to float around in my head. Now, however, was not the time to play detective. "Listen. I live just over on Blue Heron Bay, and I have enough room for you all, if you'd like to spend the night."

Both girls looked relieved at this offer, but Mrs. Henderson shook her head. "That's sweet of you dear," she said, putting her arm around Mollie, "But to tell you the truth I'd feel better over at the Lodge for the night. There's so much to think about, and frankly, I don't think any of us feels particularly safe on the lake right now."

The shrill wail of the sheriff's siren sounded in the distance, and soon the orange and white boat could be seen rounding Cedar Point, its red and white lights blinking furiously in the dark. A rather large crowd had gathered to watch the dying embers of what just a short time ago had been a lovely wood home. People stood by with buckets of water, ready to douse any flare-ups, but the fire was putting itself out as quickly as it had arisen.

"Would somebody move one of those boats, so I can dock here?" Sheriff Booker sounded grumpy, and I expected he'd been in bed when the news of the fire reached him. It had been a long day for a lot of people, the sheriff included.

"We were just leaving," I offered. "Listen, if you guys need anything, give me a call. I've got some extra jeans and sweatshirts that might get you through a day or so. Here's my number." I dug one of my new business cards out of the cockpit and handed it to Mrs. Henderson.

"A private investigator?" she said, squinting at the card. "In Cedar Hills? Well I guess you never know when or where trouble will strike." An astute observation, considering.

Erica and I climbed into the boat, and as I was getting ready to shove off, Mollie came and put her small, smudged hand on top of mine. She was a miniature version of her sister, with long blonde pigtails and an engaging grin.

"I knew you'd catch me," she said, her eyes bright and intelligent. "I was hardly scared at all. I mean it was obvious you knew what you were doing. As soon as I saw you running up the path, I knew it would be okay. Thanks."

"Hey, you're welcome, champ. You did real good. A lot of kids would've been scared to jump. You were very brave."

"Well, the alternatives weren't very appealing," she said.

This from a nine-year-old kid. Not just brave, I thought, but articulate.

"Are you leaving or not?" Sheriff Booker barked.

"See you later, kiddo," I said, winking at her. She winked right back and I eased past the other boats, waving at Sheriff Booker, who waved back despite his obvious foul mood. The Hendersons waved too, standing in a sad little cluster on their dock, surrounded by neighbors they didn't know, the skeleton of their house an eerie backdrop to a pitiful scene.

Chapter Six

That night I slept soundly and didn't wake until the sounds and smells of someone making coffee invaded my senses. It was a lovely feeling, all snuggled up in a warm bed, two cats purring like Mack trucks beside me, while someone else tinkered about in my kitchen. After a while, though, guilt began to chip away at my serenity, and when the smell of bacon wafted into my room, I found myself nearly leaping out of bed. It was after nine! How I had slept through Erica banging about in the kitchen was beyond me.

The main part of my house was essentially one huge room. There were no walls to separate the living room from the kitchen, and large glass windows and sliding glass doors provided lake views from every angle, adding to the open feeling. A large brick fireplace took up most of the only real wall in the room, and above the mantel were the bookcases I'd built myself to accommodate my growing collection of fiction. From where I stood in the hallway, I could see Erica fussing about in the kitchen.

She stood with her back to me, working at the counter, her shiny black hair still wet from the shower. She was dressed in faded jeans and a royal blue pullover sweater that matched her eyes. When she saw me I blushed, realizing that I'd been staring.

"Coffee?" she asked, grinning.

"I'd love some," I said. "Can everything else hold for a few minutes? I feel grimy from last night, and my hair smells like smoke."

"I know what you mean," she said. "I helped myself to the shower. I'll put this stuff in the oven to keep warm. Take your time."

It had been a long time since I'd appraised myself in the mirror. Living alone, I'd become somewhat complacent, if not indifferent to my own appearance, but that morning I found myself scrutinizing my reflection. I wore my hair short, not because people said it suited me, but because it was convenient and easy to care for. It had been ages since I'd worn any makeup, although in the winter when my tan began to fade, I sometimes sported a little blush on my cheeks. In the summer, the sun streaked my golden hair with the blonde highlights I'd had as a kid. My daily trek through Cedar Hills, along with the physical labor of living alone on the lake, had kept my body fairly lean and well-muscled. I didn't think anyone was going to nominate me for Playmate of the Year, but I liked the way I looked and knew that others found me attractive. I stepped into the steaming hot shower and let the water pound away at my shoulders.

Remembering Erica's breakfast, I dressed quickly. The sky outside was filled with slate-colored clouds, so I pulled on a royal blue sweater, realizing too late that I had dressed as Erica's twin. Oh, well, I thought, chuckling. She wasn't the only one who could show off her blue eyes.

Breakfast was already on the table, and we both dug in.

"This is delicious," I said, stuffing another bite into my mouth. "I usually just eat toast for breakfast."

"Well, I wouldn't want you fading away. You look like you could stand to put on some weight." She gave me a deliberate once-over. I felt myself blush at her bold appraisal, feeling her eyes on me even after I looked away.

"Actually," I said, "I eat like a horse. Martha says I was put on earth to torment her. She watches me eat, and she gains weight."

"But some women look good filled out," she said. "I thought your friend was very attractive."

"Hmm. I think that was a mutual sentiment." There! I'd said it. I half expected her to get up, proclaim her devout heterosexuality, and bolt for the door. Instead she laughed, her eyes crinkling at the corners. "What's so funny?" I asked, taking another piece of bacon.

"You are," she said. "I've been trying to figure you out since we met. Your friend Martha was easy to figure, but I wasn't sure about you." This made me laugh, since I'd been trying to figure the same thing out about her.

"What makes you so sure, now?"

"Oh, a couple of things. The way you were looking at me earlier, for one thing. And the way you blushed when I caught you checking me out."

"I was *not* checking you out," I said.

"Yes you were," she said. "And just now, when I was checking *you* out, you blushed again."

"Maybe I just blush a lot," I said, blushing.

"No, you don't. I have a feeling you haven't blushed in years."

"Can we change the subject?" I got up to put my dishes in the sink. My heart was pounding like some silly schoolgirl, with a bad crush. I wished I could just run out of the room and hide.

"Hey," Erica said, coming up behind me. She put her hand on my shoulder, and turned me to face her. "I apologize. I didn't mean to put you on the spot."

"It's okay," I said, avoiding her eyes.

"No. It's not. I don't usually come on so strong. Honest. Can we just erase the last five minutes. Start over?"

I looked into her impossibly blue eyes, and my stomach somersaulted. "I don't think so." I tore my gaze away from hers and moved her hand from my shoulder. The jolt of electricity that surged through me when I touched her hand nearly knocked me over. I dropped it immediately and worked at regaining my composure. This woman had me off balance, and I was overwhelmed by a sense of falling, which terrified me. I also kept picturing Martha, her big brown eyes beaming at Erica with obvious interest, and wondered if I was out of line.

"I'm going to go find out how the Hendersons are doing and take them some clothes," I said, moving away. "Then I'm going to go out and do a little investigating. Feel free to make yourself at home. Or, if you like, I can drop you somewhere for the day."

"If it's all right with you," she said, following me into the living room, "I'd rather come along with you. I promise I won't get in the way. It's just that I can't stand the thought of sitting around with nothing to do. Who knows? Maybe I can even be of some help." She smiled irresistibly, and against my better judgment, I agreed. Inside, I was torn between an intense desire to be close to her and an even stronger urge to flee. So I did what I always do when faced with inner turmoil. I used humor to mask my feelings.

"As long as you remember which one of us is Sherlock and which one is Holmes." It was pretty lame, but we both laughed like it was hilarious, and the tension between us dissipated a bit.

On the way over, I began to wonder if the fire and Walter Trinidad's murder were somehow related. I just didn't believe in coincidences. Jake had told me at least a dozen times to be wary of things that looked out of place. 'If you walk by the fridge and get a whiff of something rotten, you don't just pass it by do you? No, you open up the door and poke around until you find out what's gone bad.' Well, if

Jake were here today, I thought, he'd probably be asking me just how common I thought it was for there to be a man killed and a house burned down a couple of days apart in Cedar Hills.

The truth was, except for a kid running away from home every now and then, not much ever happened in the way of crime. And for some reason, I just couldn't help thinking that the Hendersons' house had been deliberately set ablaze. I kept picturing that boat I'd seen leaving in the dark, and the funny little dots hovering above it like fireflies. I closed my eyes, trying to better visualize the image of the orange dots, alternately glowing fiercer and then dying back, and suddenly I knew what I'd seen. Cigarettes!

I tried to remember how many there were and finally settled on three or four. Meaning there were at least three, maybe four people in that boat. But I just didn't see arson as a group activity. I pondered the unlikelihood of this scenario, when suddenly the thought that had been eluding me since yesterday came floating into focus.

"Your uncle didn't smoke, did he?" I asked Erica.

"Are you kidding! He was a devout non-smoker. The kind that waved his hands in the air every time anyone lit up within a block of him. At least that's how he used to be. I don't imagine he would have changed much."

"Well, according to the bartender at the Loggers Tavern, he hadn't changed at all. He went to the bar once, paid a hundred dollars to run a bar tab, then never returned because he said the bar was too smoky." I decided to skip the part about the local boys tying one on in her uncle's honor, using the credit on his bar tab to fund their celebration.

"Why do you ask?" she said.

"Well, yesterday I noticed a cigarette ash on your uncle's speedboat. At the time I thought the ash seemed out of place, because the boat was so immaculate. It never occurred to me that he didn't smoke. Considering that he was last seen leaving in that boat, and that it was returned to his dock, presumably after he'd been killed, I think it's safe to say that whoever returned the boat was smoking at the time."

"So, my uncle's killer is a smoker."

"Which narrows it down to about half the people in town." Somehow this discovery didn't cheer me.

"But at least now we have a connection between the fire and my uncle's murder," she said. "I mean, it might be flimsy, but it's something."

"Flimsy is not the word for it," I said. "Let's see what the sheriff's got. If we're right, and the people in the boat *were* prowling around the Hendersons' house . . ." I shrugged. Mary had said she'd heard voices, and if there was a connection between the fire and the murder, then I could be looking for more than one killer.

"A pack of fire-starting killers," Erica said, giggling at the absurdity.

"A den of murderous pyromaniacs."

"Who smoke like fiends," she added. By the time we pulled up to the Hendersons' dock, we were both laughing like idiots.

We were quickly sobered, however, by the sight of the blackened hulk that had once been the

Hendersons' home. It was even more gruesome in daylight than it had been in the dead of night. The air was thick with a stench reminiscent of singed hair, and from the dock I could see the Hendersons, Sheriff Booker and others milling about, rummaging through the debris for salvageable remains. Erica and I climbed out of the boat, and she handed me the bundle of old clothes we'd put together before we left.

"Mom! It's the detectives!" Mollie called out, loping down the walkway to meet us. Her long blonde hair was tied up in pigtails, and she wore brand new, bright pink sweats already smeared with charcoal.

"The lady in the lodge went and bought us all new jogging suits from the hardware store," she said, twirling around for us to admire her new duds. "Daddy paid, of course, but it was a nice gesture, don't you think?"

"It certainly was," I agreed. Mrs. Henderson came toward us, hefting a metal filing box that had survived the heat, and set it beside the other rescued items on the ground. She was wearing a gaudy turquoise sweat suit that fit a bit too snugly but which was probably preferable to the nightgown she'd worn the night before. Her light brown hair was pulled back with a lime green scarf, revealing a round, attractive face, slightly smudged with soot. I handed her the bag of clothes I'd brought and said, "If there's anything here you can use, feel free to borrow it. You can return them when you've had a chance to get things in order again."

She looked at me and then Erica, and tears welled up, spilling down her cheeks. "Everyone has

60

been so darned nice," she said, swiping at her tears. "I guess it takes something horrible to happen to realize how lucky we really are."

"What's the sheriff say?" I asked. "Any idea what caused the fire?"

She sighed. "He says it was arson. There were two gas cans left out back. He also found several footprints, all different ones, so he thinks there may have been more than one person involved."

Erica and I exchanged glances, but said nothing.

"Now, that's odd," Mrs. Henderson said, walking past us down the walkway.

"What's odd?" I asked.

"Well, I've been by this spot a dozen times this morning, but I just noticed, our sign is missing."

"What kind of sign?" I asked.

"We had it hand-made. It says 'Hendersons' Hideaway.' The fire didn't come this far. I wonder what happened to it?"

"Maybe your husband already took it down," Erica suggested.

"Maybe." She sounded doubtful. She headed back to the ruined house as Sheriff Booker sauntered down to where we stood, his silver hair blowing in the breeze.

"Cassidy James. I've seen more of you in two days than in two whole years!" he said, sounding much more cheerful than he had the previous night.

"Well, you don't seem particularly pleased about it," I teased.

"On the contrary. From what I hear, you gals pretty much saved that little girl's life. You just happen to be passing by last night, or what?"

"I was taking Ms. Trinidad back to my place, like

I told you on the phone. Listen Sheriff, you believe in a little quid pro quo?"

"You mean, like I scratch your back, you scratch mine?"

"Something like that," I said. "It just seems that as long as we keep bumping into each other, we may as well work together."

"Don't tell me someone has hired you to look into this fire?"

"Well, no," I admitted, fumbling for words. "But I do think this fire may be connected to Trinidad's murder. So the fire might be relevant."

Sheriff Booker put his arm around my shoulders and steered me down toward the dock. "Now, Cassie, you know damned well that in matters of the law it's your duty to report any suspicions you might have to an officer of the law, which in this case is me. Now, what makes you think this fire is in any way, shape or form connected to Walter Trinidad's murder?"

Taking a deep breath, I told him about the ashes on Trinidad's boat, and the boat we'd seen leaving the Hendersons' the night before with three or maybe four people in it, all smoking.

"Did you get a look at the type of boat, Cass? Color, shape, size, anything at all?"

"It rode low in the water. No cabin. Like a bass boat, maybe. But it could have been an aluminum motorboat or even a speedboat. It was very dark, and like I said, they didn't have any lights on. The only way we know there were at least three people was because of the cigarettes."

Sheriff Booker stroked his silver moustache thoughtfully, peering up at the clouds as if they held some answer. The day was turning. chilly, and I suspected it would be raining soon.

"Well," he said at last. "That's very interesting indeed. See, I found a whole mess of footprints around the house back there. And they're all different sizes. Of course, we had people stomping around here last night from all over, so it's going to take a miracle to sort them all out, but it's a place to start, isn't it?"

"Wouldn't there be a difference in the prints left before and after the fire?" I asked. "I mean, it seems like the ashes would be on top of any prints left before the fire was set, whereas the prints left by the neighbors should be on top of the ashes."

Sheriff Booker flashed me such a beatific smile that had I been straight, it would probably have melted my heart. Even over fifty, he was undoubtedly the handsomest man I'd ever actually known.

"I wish I'd thought of that two hours ago," he said. "By God, you may just have something there, Miz James. It's pretty trampled over, but we just might find something we can use. I hope you're right." He bustled back up the walkway at a brisk clip, and I followed after him. "But as far as your theory about any connection between this and the Trinidad case," he said over his shoulder, "well, personally I think you're full of beans. Unless you can find me something more solid than the fact that smoking was involved in both cases, I'm afraid I've got to look at these as completely separate and unrelated incidents."

He was right, and I knew it. I watched him hurry back to the side of the house, kneeling on the ground inspecting footprints. Mrs. Henderson came out empty handed and I imagined that anything worth saving had already been dragged out to the front yard. It wasn't much, I thought, inspecting the sorry heap of unburned remnants. But at least no one had been hurt.

"He says he didn't take it down," she said.

"I beg your pardon?"

"My husband. He says he noticed the sign missing first thing this morning. He has no idea where it is. I can't believe someone would steal our sign. The girls haven't seen it either."

"Maybe one of the neighbors . . ." I left the sentence hanging. The thought that a neighbor would steal a sign in the wake of such a disaster was unthinkable. And besides, who would want a sign with someone else's name on it?

I again offered the use of my house, but Mrs. Henderson again declined, saying the sooner she could get off the lake, the better. I had a feeling that Cedar Hills may have just lost a nice family as residents. Before leaving, I wanted to talk to Mollie, just to make sure she wasn't suffering from too much stress after the harrowing event the night before. As we walked back to my boat, she assured me that she was fine.

"It's my mom I worry about," she said. "Dad will be fine. The insurance should cover the cost of rebuilding. But I'm afraid mom is all freaked over this. She thinks someone is out to get us."

"What do you think?" I asked.

"I think that rotten Alan Pinkerton had something to do with it!"

"Alan Pinkerton? Who's Alan Pinkerton?"

Her sister came up behind us, startling me when she spoke. "Oh puh-leeze, don't go into that again, Mollie. I swear, you're like a broken record."

"What's she talking about?" I asked Mary, who like the others, was wearing new sweats. Hers were pale blue and matched her eyes.

"She thinks this boy I dated *one* time, and one time only, was so possessed with desire for my body that he came and burned our house down when I refused to go out with him again."

"Well, he did call you about two million times!" Mollie said defiantly.

"I'm so sure!" Mary shot back. "I mean, can you believe it? My sister has an overactive imagination."

"You could be right," I said, feeling miserable at the look of betrayal Mollie gave me when I said it. "But you never know," I tried to appease her. "Two million phone calls, huh? The boy must be in love."

"The creep, you mean," Mollie said. "Half the time he just hangs up. Or breathes funny. Or whispers, 'Mary, Mary, Mary.' He's a certified perv."

"Oh, Mollie," Mary said.

"When's the last time he called you?" I asked.

"Last night," Mary said. "My dad answered the phone and told him to quit bothering us or he'd call the cops. It *was* getting kind of bothersome, but it was harmless, really. I mean, the guy is on the football team. It's not like he was hard up or anything. I think he just wasn't used to girls saying no."

"Yeah," Mollie piped up. "It crushed his frail, male ego."

I had to admit, I liked this kid, active imagination and all. "Well, it's worth checking out, anyway," I said, climbing aboard my boat. "If you think of anything else, give me a call." Erica shoved us away from the dock, and we sped off, leaving Mary to argue with her peculiarly intelligent and insistent little sister.

Chapter Seven

The rain began to fall softly as we pulled up to the marina. Tommy, wearing cutoffs and a T-shirt, didn't seem to notice the weather change. Grinning as I eased into a vacant slip, he continued hammering the bright white dock bumpers into place. The long-awaited bumpers had finally arrived.

"Mornin', ladies," he said, his teeth clamped around a half-smoked cigarette. That's funny, I thought, I'd never seen Tommy smoking before. Maybe it was just that I suddenly had smoking on the brain.

"Good morning, Tommy. What's new?"

"New bumpers come in," he said, stating the obvious. "Also, there was a big fire last night out at Pebble Cove. I didn't see it, but they say it burned down the whole house. Oh, and Meg Simpson had her baby last night. A little girl."

"Tommy, you are a veritable wealth of information today," I said. "Any idea when and where the football team practices?" Erica looked at me sideways, and I shrugged. I didn't have anything better to go on. Why not?

"In the summer?" Tommy asked. "They don't usually hold no formal practice until mid-August. But some of the guys scrimmage over at the school on their own. Might be there now, seein' as it's Saturday. Then again, they're just as likely to be sleepin' in, or off fishin' somewhere. The bass are running pretty hot right now. I caught me a real beaut last night."

"Oh really? Where was that?" I asked, thinking about Tommy's boat. It was a royal blue speedboat that rode low in the water and as far as I knew, it didn't even have running lights. It could maybe carry three passengers besides the driver, but it would be a tight fit.

"Oh, now, Cass. I can't tell you that. It's the bass fisherman's law. You never give away a good fishin' hole."

"But isn't it dangerous?" I tried to be nonchalant. "Driving at night with no lights?"

"Nah, I do it all the time. Easier to sneak up on the fish that way." Tommy's eyes crinkled with mischief.

"I'm surprised you didn't see the fire, then." I ignored Erica's raised eyebrows.

"Well, even if I had've seen it, there wasn't nothin' we coulda done about it. From what I hear tell, it got burnt down to the ground just like that." He snapped his fingers for emphasis.

"Then you weren't out all by yourself?" I asked, trying not to sound like I was interrogating him. After all, I considered Tommy Green a friend.

"Well, actually, if you want to know the truth," Tommy said, blushing slightly, "I was out with a lady friend. We didn't really do all that much fishin'."

Call me a skeptic, but I get nervous when someone says they're about to tell the truth. Still, the blush looked real. "Not that pretty little gal I saw you flirting with last week at McGregors?" I asked, doing a little fishing of my own. Tommy's blue eyes narrowed, and he tossed his cigarette into the lake.

"I don't kiss and tell, Cassidy. That's one of my rules." He scrunched up his face in an attempt to look stern, though the result was more comical than menacing. Even so, I decided it was time to ease off.

"Okay, Tommy. Your secret's safe with me," I said, hoping the joke would mask any suspicion in my voice. I tossed Erica an extra rain jacket from the boat and led her up the ramp.

"You suspect him, don't you?" she whispered.

"I don't know," I admitted. "Right now, I'm not ruling anyone out."

"Even me?" She slipped the rain jacket over her shapely body. It was amazing, I thought, that anyone could look that good in a rain jacket.

"Even you," I said, pulling my own jacket over my head. I wasn't sure, though, if I meant it or not.

Living on a lake in Oregon, I hadn't taken long to equip my car, boat and house with plenty of rain gear. Umbrellas were used only in extreme weather, and opening one in a mild mist like this would be a sure sign to all who passed that here walked a Southern Californian. I explained this to Erica as we began our jaunt in the rain.

"There seems to be a lot of anti-California sentiment around here," she noted. I wasn't sure, but she may have been pouting over my comment about suspecting her.

"Probably not much more here than elsewhere," I said, glad she didn't choose to pursue the other topic. "It seems to be a common feeling east and north of California, kind of like the way so many Europeans dislike Americans. I don't know if it's envy because of all the sunshine, or distrust because of the liberal lifestyles. Some of it's legitimate anger. Californians have more money to spend. They sell their houses in California for two or three hundred thousand and come up here to live dirt cheap. Compared to the locals, they're rich. They drive nicer cars, wear more fashionable clothes and buy bigger boats. On top of that, they complain incessantly about the rain. And worst of all, they try to change things. They expect the service in restaurants and stores to be faster, the choices bigger and the quality better. Everyone who's not a Californian is treated like some kind of country bumpkin. It's not surprising that people resent the invasion."

"It's funny," Erica said as we made our way through the streets of Cedar Hills, "you keep saying 'they' and 'them,' but you're from California yourself, right?"

"That's true. I guess ideologically I'm somewhere in between. I like the slow pace here, and the people.

I like the trees and fresh air. I don't miss the violence or the smog. I like myself better too. I'm not in so much of a hurry anymore. I'm more relaxed. But there're times I still feel like an outsider. People here treat me warmly, but I'm not sure how receptive some of them would be if they knew my sexual orientation."

"Then what do you do for a social life?" Erica asked. "I assume there aren't a lot of opportunities for gays and lesbians in Cedar Hills."

I paused, thinking. "Not in Cedar Hills, true. But there's a pretty big lesbian community in Ashland and Portland, from what I hear. Even Kings Harbor has some outlets. Martha is always trying to get me to participate in all sorts of activities. Golf tournaments, dances, softball leagues. And I know they've got at least one gay bar. I guess I just haven't been real interested so far. But it's nice knowing it's there if I change my mind."

"Hmm. Maybe when this whole thing is over, we'll have to go check it out. Maybe your friend Martha could take us." She smiled, and I felt what was becoming an all-too-familiar sensation in the pit of my stomach.

By now we'd walked to the far end of Main Street, and as we rounded the corner, Cedar Hills School rose up in front of us, an orange and green monstrosity that sprawled across the better part of five acres. I'd passed it many times but had never felt compelled to set foot on the grounds. Having taught junior high school for six years, I'd had my fill of screaming adolescents. Don't get me wrong. I liked teaching. But having left the profession, I had no desire to return to it.

The school itself was far too big for the town of Cedar Hills, even though it housed grades kindergarten through twelve. Built in the days when Cedar Hills thrived as a bustling logging town, it had much more room than it needed for the few hundred students who attended.

"You really think this kid, Alan Pinkerton, might have had something to do with the fire?" Erica asked. "I thought you were just humoring the little girl."

"Well, actually, I was. But it's worth a quick rule-out. Besides, it's such a nice day for a walk."

Erica laughed, because by that time, we were both fairly soaked, despite our rain jackets. We ducked under the covered hallways, avoiding the puddles forming beneath downspouts. Here and there the walls were adorned with colorful renditions of the school mascot, the Cedar Hills Duck, a rather sinister cousin of Daffy. Ahead of us, a custodial cart was parked in an open doorway and as we neared, a man with a gray stubbled beard and a Mariners cap was dumping the contents of a dust pan into the metal trash bin on his cart.

"Excuse me," I said. "Can you point us in the direction of the football field?"

He peered at us over horn-rimmed glasses and pointed east, the direction we were already headed.

"Looks like you had a little accident," I said, noticing the broken glass he was dumping into the bin.

72

"Damn vandals," he said. "Messed up the whole science room."

"Really? When was this?"

"Beats me." He shrugged. "Coulda been last night, or any time after Tuesday. That was the last time I did this hallway. It was all right then. Look at it now."

He stepped aside. Erica and I peeked into the room. Chairs and tables were toppled over, and broken glass was everywhere. A punched-in window on the opposite wall showed the obvious point of entrance, and on the green chalk board was a giant, block-style swastika.

"Any idea who'd do something like this?" I asked.

The man looked at me more closely. "Do I know you?" he asked. "I don't recall seeing you around here before. I'm Earl Bean, Head Custodian."

Erica and I introduced ourselves, and because it was becoming a habit, I handed him one of my calling cards.

"A private investigator, eh? Well, good. Maybe you can catch the ones that done this. I'd like to get my hands on 'em myself."

"Has this happened before?" I asked, moving into the classroom and walking around carefully. A lot of broken glass had come from containers holding chemicals, and the odors in the room were unpleasant. I hoped there wasn't a deadly mixture amid the seeping fluids congealing on the floor.

"Never like this," he replied. "We sometimes get a little graffiti on the walls. These damn swastikas been showing up real regular. Now and then we get a busted window. But this here was deliberate and nasty. Look what they done to the frogs." He stepped into a small alcove off the main room and I followed. On the table were at least a dozen dead frogs reeking of formaldehyde. The frogs were positioned in various stages of fornication, some showing remarkable originality.

"Cute," I said.

"Disgusting if you ask me. Look at this one. Someone musta wanted frog legs for dinner." Sure enough, someone had rendered the poor frog a paraplegic.

Erica came up behind us. "At least *this* room wasn't trashed."

"I wonder what they did with the formaldehyde?"

"What do you mean?" Erica asked.

"Well, formaldehyde has a very distinctive odor. There are a lot of chemicals spilled out there, but I'd bet my last dollar not one of them is formaldehyde. And I don't see any in here either. Which means, whoever did this took the frogs out of their container and then took the container of formaldehyde with them."

The three of us began searching the science lab for any container that might have held the frogs in formaldehyde, and it soon became clear that my suspicions were right. Unless the frogs had jumped up there by themselves, engaged in an amphibious orgy and then died from the exertion, someone had made off with a container of formaldehyde.

"They're lucky they didn't blow the place to smithereens," the custodian said.

"Why is that?" I asked.

"Because with all those chemicals, and them smoking right here in the room, they coulda blown their heads off." Little bells began ringing in my head. "What makes you think they were smoking?" I asked.

"The butts," he said. "I found two of 'em right over there by the window."

"Can I see them?" My heart started to do little pirouettes.

"I already swept 'em up, but you're welcome to look in the bin."

Risking lacerating my wrists on broken shards, I gingerly picked my way through the debris until I found the two cigarette butts amid the rubble. One was only half smoked. It was a Marlboro. I carefully wrapped them in a tissue, which I replaced in my jacket pocket.

"This is getting weird," Erica murmured.

"It's probably just a coincidence," I said.

"I thought you didn't believe in coincidence," she teased.

"I don't."

We went back in to help pick up the tables and chairs, but Mr. Bean waved us off. "You gals go on now. I can finish up here. But promise me if you catch the rascals that done this, you'll give 'em the what for."

For some reason I couldn't explain, I wasn't anxious to leave. I walked around the perimeter of the room, searching — for what, I didn't know. And then I saw it.

"Look!" I said, pointing to the broken window. Like a tiny flag waving in the breeze, a small triangle of green nylon clung precariously to the sharp edge of the protruding glass. I quickly pulled one of the student desks over to the window, and balancing myself somewhat awkwardly, I managed to free the shred of nylon.

"Looks like one of them school jackets," Mr. Bean said, peering at the small piece of cloth. "I got one of them myself, and it looks just about like that. 'Course, practically everyone in town's got one of them jackets, so it probably ain't gonna be much help."

"Maybe so, Mr. Bean," I said, refusing to let his pessimism ruin my good mood. "But not everyone in town has got a jacket with a little hole torn out of it, now do they?"

"You got a point there, missy," he said, chewing his lower lip. He resumed pushing the broken glass into small piles, and Erica and I left him to his endeavors, making our way to the football field, which was deserted. The rain had begun to come down in earnest, and even the hardiest of local boys had sense enough to take cover from the onslaught. Disappointed, Erica and I huddled beneath an overhang, waiting for it to let up before we ventured back toward the marina.

"Okay," I said, "let me run this by you, and you tell me if I'm missing anything. First, your uncle is lured away from home, murdered, his penis cut off and his body dumped in the lake. His boat's returned to his dock and someone, presumably the killer, leaves a cigarette ash on the edge of the boat. Someone also may or may not have entered his room while you were sleeping. Everyone in town hates him so it's not hard to imagine someone getting mad enough to kill him. So far, so good?"

"I'm with you," she said.

"Okay. Next, someone sets the Hendersons' house on fire. We think there may be more than one person involved because there were at least three, maybe four cigarettes lit up in a boat leaving the scene. Unlike your uncle, the Hendersons are generally well-liked. No enemies, except maybe a love-sick teenager, who a nine-year-old tells us is weird, and who makes crank calls to the older sister. Not exactly a likely suspect for arson and murder."

"Except I also got two crank calls," Erica interjected. "So at least we have another possible connection between the two crimes."

"Exactly. So, for lack of a better idea, we head over to the school in hopes of getting a look at this crank caller who might be playing football in the rain, and instead we find a vandalized science room. Aside from the fact that crime of any kind is rare in this town, and this happens to be the third incident in as many days, there's nothing at all to suggest that the vandalism has anything to do with the fire or the murder. Except that once again we find evidence of cigarettes at the scene. This time we get lucky and actually have the brand, which could narrow it down some. But the connection is still extremely thin. What we do know is that there was more than one vandal, and that at least two of them smoke, and that one of them is walking around with a little hole torn out of his green shirt or jacket."

"And they're into Hitler," Erica said. "Did you see the size of that swastika? That took some time."

"Right. What we don't know is if they have anything at all to do with the other crimes. What else?"

"Well, just out of curiosity, did you happen to

notice what brand of cigarette Tommy was smoking at the marina?"

I nodded, unhappy with the answer. "Marlboro," I said. "But here's what's really bothering me. Think about this. Why did someone break into the science lab in the first place? To make dead frogs hump? No. To get some formaldehyde. And what do you do with formaldehyde? You preserve dead things with it. So the question is, who would suddenly have a need to preserve a dead thing?" I waited patiently, hating the image I was painting for her. Suddenly she got it and her face turned slightly green.

"Oh, God," she said. "I can't believe I didn't think of that. Whoever cut off my uncle's penis wanted to preserve it. Like a trophy? For God's sake. I think I'm going to be sick."

"You and me both." We stood watching the rain pound the ground around us. Several moments passed without either of us speaking. Finally, I said, "This really could connect the crimes. The arson may be totally unrelated, but it's possible the murderer is also the one who broke in to get the formaldehyde. Which means we might really have some concrete evidence. I think we better talk to Sheriff Booker before we do another thing."

The rain had begun to let up and we hurried back to the marina. Our fronts were kept relatively dry by the rain jackets, but my hood kept slipping off, allowing water to pour down my neck, soaking my back and plastering my hair to my head. We were halfway back when a beat-up green pickup rambled up beside us.

"You ladies like a lift?" Jess flashed a crooked grin. Erica and I scrambled into his moldy front seat, grateful for the refuge, and I introduced the two of them. "How's the detective work going?" he asked, his green eyes smiling.

"Like a wild goose chase," I said. "The more I look into one thing, the more I find something out about another thing. And nothing seems to fit together. I'm beginning to wonder about my detective skills."

"Oh, now, Cassie. You don't give yourself enough credit. You just hardly got started. If it's any consolation, I hear Sheriff Booker and that tight ass Grimes have been scratching their heads a lot too. I'm sure between you, you'll figure it out."

"Well, I'm glad someone has confidence in me, anyway. Hey, listen, not to change the subject, but do you happen to know a kid named Alan Pinkerton?" I asked.

Jess looked at me quizzically, tucking his long hair behind his ears.

"Sure do. He's on the football team with Dougie. Why do you want to know?" Jess's truck was still running, but we sat idling at the curb.

"Oh, no reason really. I just heard his name and couldn't put a face to it."

"Well, I'm sure you've seen him around. Big, good-looking kid. Blond, real light blue eyes. He's the running back. Not a lot of speed, but he's big and can bowl them over real good. You seen any of the games?"

I told Jess I hadn't had that pleasure.

"Oh, it ain't much of a pleasure. Last year they went one and seven. Not enough boys to really make a team. Most of them play both ways. Even Dougie, who's too small to be playing in the first place. I thought it would do him some good to be on a team. Teach him responsibility, you know? But if anything, he's gotten worse." Jess had been having trouble with his son since I'd known him.

"He still stealing from you?" The kid had been pilfering small change and beer from the house last time I'd heard.

"Not since I caught him red-handed. I swear to you, Cass, I don't believe in hitting kids, but I damn near knocked him across the room that day. Not only was he standing there going through my wallet, but he had the nerve to lie to my face. Now neither he or his mother is speaking to me. I'll tell you one thing. The day he turns eighteen can't come soon enough."

"How's little Jess?" I asked, referring to Jess's ten-year-old daughter, Jessica, who'd spent the better part of a week last summer helping me put in a vegetable garden. I'd paid her handsomely, and we'd both enjoyed each other's company, working side by side digging in the dirt, the hot sun tanning our backs. She'd asked a million questions about what it was like to be a private eye, and had shown a healthy curiosity about everything around her. A neat little kid.

"She's doin' real good. Got her own lawn mowing route and is squirreling away money faster than her old man. Even opened her own bank account the other day." Pride glowed on Jess's face. Little Jess was the spitting image of Jess himself, with long brown hair she wore in a ponytail like her dad's, and big green eyes that looked even bigger behind her wire-frame glasses. At ten, she hadn't gotten tall yet, but you could tell from her gangly frame that she was going to shoot up any day now. Jess's son Doug, on the other hand, was short and stout. Jess never said so, but I suspected the boy he'd raised as his own son had been sired by someone else. There was no question, however, about the parentage of little Jessie. She was a miniature version of her father.

"You hear any good gossip lately?" I asked, changing the subject.

"Yeah. I hear you and your lady friend here saved some little girl's life on Pebble Cove last night. Nice goin'."

"It was all Cass," Erica said, patting my knee. "She's real calm in an emergency."

"Oh, yeah," Jess said, teasing. "I saw her jump up on the sofa screaming her head off when one of those cats of hers drug a mouse into the living room. Real brave, our Miz James."

"It was a rat!" I said, laughing with them. Erica gave my knee the lightest squeeze before moving her hand away. I felt the heat rush up, reddening my cheeks and sending disturbing signals to parts of my body I hadn't acknowledged in a long while. I turned to look out the window.

"Doesn't look like it's going to let up any time soon," I said. "You want to drop us off at McGregors? I need to make some phone calls and do some shopping."

"At your service." Jess drove the few blocks to the grocery store. Erica offered to start on the groceries while I dialed Sheriff Booker's office from the pay phone outside of McGregors. Naturally he was out, but I left a message with his secretary to call me ASAP, and then I called Martha.

"Make it quick, kiddo. I'm up to my ears in paperwork," she said.

"Hello to you, too. What's the status on the phone tap on Trindad's place?"

"No go. That asshole Grimes vetoed the order. Accused me of interfering with his investigation. He also says he's been looking all over Kingdom Come for his prime suspect, a certain Ms. Trinidad. He thinks she's avoiding him." Martha's laugh was bitter. "I don't think he's very fond of you either," she added.

"My heart is broken. Hey, I've got some stuff I want to run by you. Any chance you can come out to the house later?"

"I don't get off until four o'clock," she said.

"I thought we'd have a light supper. Maybe start off with a crab and avocado cocktail, work our way into some linguini alfredo, with perhaps a small pork chop, lightly sautéed . . ."

"Stop already! I'll be there! God, you really know the way to a woman's heart. I won't be able to work now, with my stomach growling." I laughed and left Martha to her paperwork.

When I stepped out of the phone booth, I paused for a moment, gazing across the street at the window of Lizzie's bar. I couldn't see in, but I knew that Lizzie, standing behind the bar, could see out. There wasn't much that went on along Main Street that Lizzie Thompson didn't know about. And the way she'd fidgeted the day before, I guessed she knew something she wasn't telling.

Making my mind up quickly, I hurried across the street and let myself into the dark, smoky interior. If I was fast, I could meet up with Erica before she finished the shopping. There were only a few customers in the bar at this time of day, and they were busy at the pool table.

"Kind of early for you, isn't it Cass?" Lizzie said, leaning on the counter. She was a big woman with rough, weathered hands and a face to match. In her forties, with gray streaks running through her short, curly hair, she could look tough, when she wanted, but when she smiled, her toothy grin reminded me of a big, old, huggable teddy bear.

"I'm not here to drink, Lizzie," I said, waving the beer glass away. "I think you know why I'm here." Lizzie's eyes narrowed, and then opened wide with innocence. I waited her out, letting her go through all the facial expressions she could muster to convey ignorance and innocence, and in the end my patience paid off. Her hands started fidgeting again, and her eyes went straight for the window. "You must see an awful lot through that window, Lizzie. Kind of like watching a soap opera. I'll bet there's all sorts of stuff you know about people in this town." I didn't expect her to capitulate quite so easily, but apparently her self-imposed guilt was more of a strain than she could bear.

"He was having an affair!" she blurted out suddenly. Then, lowering her voice, with a quick glance at the pool table, she went on. "I pride myself, Cassidy, on being the only soul in this whole damn town who does *not* spend the whole day gossiping. I listen, like any good bartender, and I see plenty, but I keep my mouth shut. People have come to know they can depend on me. They trust me with their secrets, they cry on my shoulder, they consider me a friend."

I nodded, knowing this was true, and understanding why divulging something secret, even about Walter Trinidad, was so difficult for her.

"I never liked the bastard myself. And what that woman saw in him is beyond me. She's as cute as a button, though from what I've gathered, Walter Trinidad was not her first, uh, outside interest."

"Who, Lizzie? For God's sake, who are we talking about here?" Patience never has actually been one of my virtues. I can fake patience, but Lizzie was stretching my acting abilities to the limit. She leaned closer, and whispered the name. Her breath smelled of cigarettes and breath mints, an interesting combination. "The postmaster's wife?" I said aloud. Lizzie shot me a pained look, and I lowered my voice. "How do you know?"

"Like you said, Cassie. I saw them with my own eyes right through this window. Two different times, he dropped her off in his Lincoln, right in front of McGregors. Anyone could have seen them. Like she was flaunting it, hoping she'd get caught."

"When was this, Lizzie?" I thought of Betty Beechcomb, a diminutive bleached blonde with fire engine red nails and ever-present three-inch spikes, trying to picture her with Walter Trinidad. Like Barbie with Godzilla, I thought.

"The first time was about three weeks ago. And then again on Tuesday. The day before he was, uh, done in. They may have been together more than that, but those were the only two times I saw them."

"Time of day?"

"The first time was about nine o'clock. Ed's in

that bowling league on Wednesday nights and they usually get out around ten. I reckon she was trying to beat him home. Then this last Tuesday, it was even later. Around eleven o'clock. I don't know where Ed was that night, or maybe he was at home thinking she was out with the girls. But in a town this small, it was only a matter of time before poor Ed would've heard about it. If I saw them together twice, you can bet someone else probably saw them too."

"Do you think maybe Ed did find out, Lizzie? Has he acted strange lately, anything like that?"

"Ed Beechcomb is a regular. Comes in a couple of times a week. Real quiet man. What I call totally P.W."

I raised my eyebrows and she grinned.

"Pussy whipped," she said, eyes twinkling. "I think little Betty could eat poor Ed alive. Sometimes I think the reason he comes in here so much is to get some rest. After working all day at the post office, he needs to get his strength up to handle what's waiting for him at home." Lizzie's eyes had lit up, and she was clearly feeling better now that she'd gotten the story off her chest. Then, looking around the bar, she seemed to realize that she'd come perilously close to engaging in gossip, and she lowered her voice. "I'd hate to see him get hurt. You know how rumors in this town can fly. I mean, it's entirely possible that there's some perfectly innocent explanation for those two being together." I could tell by her eyes she didn't believe it any more than I did.

"I'll keep this completely to myself, Lizzie," I said.

"Thank you. It may be nothing, but it's definitely something that should be looked into. You did the right thing."

She heaved a sigh, clearly relieved at having rid herself of the burden. Her smile exposed her slightly protruding teeth and with a shock, I realized that she was suddenly looking at me flirtatiously. Good ol' Lizzie Thompson, who could arm-wrestle any man in town, was giving me the eye.

I grinned back, with what I hoped was a combination of acknowledgment and appreciation without the least amount of encouragement. As I walked out, I wasn't sure I had succeeded.

By the time I rushed into McGregors, Erica was nearly done with the shopping.

"I forgot to tell you to get some bread," I said, slightly out of breath. She smiled and held up a long loaf of sourdough.

"You also forgot to mention fresh parmesan. Fear not." She showed me the cart, brimming with such a varied array of goodies that I laughed aloud. There were bags of potato chips, a box of brownie mix, large slabs of various cheeses, a jar of lumpfish caviar, several bottles of Oregon wine including an excellent Pinot Gris that had just come out and a dozen other delectables hidden beneath.

"You did remember the pork chops?" I asked, half kidding.

She smiled, her blue eyes flashing with merriment, and led the way to the check-out counter.

Erica insisted on paying for the groceries and after a few minutes I gave up arguing. Behind us, we heard a sudden commotion and turned in time to see

Jess's son, Dougie, chasing hard after his younger sister. Dougie was more than twice as big as Jessie, with thick, bowed legs and a barrel chest. He had a wrestler's body, along with a thick neck and squarish face. His hair was long in front, with brown bangs hanging down his forehead, but in back, his head was neatly shaved. I watched in disgust as Dougie caught up to little Jess, who had nearly made it out the door. Grabbing her long ponytail, Dougie yanked Jessie backwards and smacked her across the head, sending her sprawling, her wire-frame glasses skidding across the floor.

"Hey! Knock it off!" I yelled. Once a teacher, always a teacher, I thought grimly, racing toward them.

Dougie looked back at me and scowled, his dark eyes narrowing. "Get lost, creep," he said. At first I thought he was addressing me, but then I saw Jessie get to her feet, retrieve her glasses and run full speed out of the store. It broke my heart to see tears pooling in her big green eyes.

"What's the matter, Dougie. Can't you find someone your own size to pick on?" I took another step toward him, my fists clenched.

He shot me a withering look and sauntered slowly out the doorway, saying nothing. I hadn't really liked Dougie before, but this little episode pretty much sealed it for me. The kid was a loser.

Back at the marina, we stopped by Erica's car, which turned out to be a bright red Miata. Erica unloaded two large suitcases from the tiny trunk and between them and the groceries, it took us several trips to load everything into the boat.

"I'm not moving in, honest," Erica said, handing me one of her bags. "I'm just tired of living out of my overnight bag."

"You never did say where you were on your way to."

"Canada. By now I should be tooling my way across beautiful British Columbia, seeing the sights."

"On your own?" I asked.

"It's a long story, but yeah, definitely on my own."

Chapter Eight

The gods and goddesses, in a rare burst of benevolence, parted the clouds for a thin but brilliant ray of sunshine while we unloaded the boat and toted our bags up to my house. Gammon and Panic were appropriately ecstatic upon our return, alternately rubbing against Erica and myself as we entered.

"How's your hot water supply?" Erica asked, taking her things down the hallway to the guest room she'd slept in.

"Fine, why?"

"Because even though I showered earlier, I'm cold and wet and would kill for a hot bath."

"Help yourself," I said. "Or if you'd prefer, you can use the hot tub out back. I keep it heated."

Erica's eyes lit up. "Really? I think I'm in heaven." She disappeared into her room and when she emerged, wearing a white terry robe that just covered her thighs, I had to catch my breath. Her skin was a satiny brown and her legs, which started somewhere under her robe, went on forever. The robe revealed a tantalizing glimpse of cleavage, and for the second time that day, I caught myself openly staring at her. "You going to join me?" she asked, returning my gaze. I was still dressed in my wet clothes, standing in the kitchen.

"Uh, no. I better not. I've got some things I need to put away here." This sounded lame, since most of the things had already been put away, but I didn't trust the fluttering in my heart.

"Oh, come on," she said. "You can't stand around in wet clothes all day. Leave what's left for later and I'll help you. Join me, okay?"

Unable to think of a convincing reason not to, I told her I'd be out in a few minutes. I heard her go through the sliding glass door as I stood staring into the sink, trying to regain my composure. It had been years since I'd even been interested in a woman and even then, it hadn't felt like this. My heart was slamming against my chest in rhythm with the little flips my stomach was doing. This is absurd, I thought. I'm acting like a lovesick adolescent. Except I knew that as an adolescent I'd never felt anything remotely close to this.

Against my better judgment, I peeled off my wet

90

clothes, pulled my own terrycloth robe around me, belting it snugly, and took two Heinekens out of the refrigerator. Outside, the steam was already rising in hot puffs around the tub, which was sunken into the redwood deck surrounded by red cedar and Douglas fir. It was a beautiful scene, made more so by the shimmering image of a woman enveloped in steam. Erica had her back to me, her bare shoulders catching the glint of sun that still poked through the clouds. Quickly, I slipped out of my robe and into the steaming water.

"This is great." She turned to face me, her cheeks already flushed by the heat. I handed her an open Heineken which she gulped gratefully before settling back into the water. I made a point of not looking beneath the water, not wanting to invade her privacy, yet intensely aware of her nakedness so close to mine.

"So, Ms. Trinidad," I said in a calm voice belying my feelings, "tell me, what exactly do you do for a living? It occurs to me that I know almost nothing about you."

She laughed. Those little crinkly lines around her eyes and her perfect white teeth did nothing to calm the dancing in my heart. "You want my whole life story, or just the salient details?"

"May as well hear the long version."

And so we talked.

Erica was thirty-five, five years my senior. A journalism major at Berkeley, she'd landed a job with *Rolling Stone* right out of college, a minor miracle in the competitive world of journalism. By twenty-five she'd written her first novel.

"It was terrible," she said. "Full of all the things

I believed in. Terribly serious. Thank God it was never published."

But from that point on she was hooked on writing, and in one of those rare moments of true inspiration, brought on, she said, by too much red wine, she decided to try her hand at romance novels.

"I never actually liked romance, myself," she said. "But I'd read somewhere how successful some of these writers were, and I thought, what the hell? So I gave it a try."

"And?"

She grinned, taking a swig of her beer. "And it turns out I'm damned good at it."

Then she told me her pen name and I about choked on my beer. "You're Sheila Gay?" I asked incredulously.

"Clever name, don't you think?"

"I can't believe it! How many books have you written?" I was dumbfounded. Even though I didn't read a lot of romance novels, I knew who Sheila Gay was.

"Counting the one I just finished, twenty-three. I could grind out more, but I like to give it a break now and then. I average about two a year."

No wonder she wasn't hurting for money.

"And you've lived alone all this time?" I asked.

"Heavens no," she said, her deep, sexy voice full of laughter. "I'll spare you the details of my youthful exploits. Let it suffice to say there is no shortage of opportunities for a young lesbian journalist working for *Rolling Stone* in San Francisco."

"I can imagine,"

"But that grew old. I finally settled down about

six years ago. Found the woman of my dreams. The real thing, you know?"

I told her I did. "And where is this lucky lady?" I asked. I knew immediately that this was the wrong question to ask.

"She passed away last year."

This was the first time I'd been on the asking end of that question, and I suddenly understood the awkwardness people must have felt when they asked me about Diane. I told her how sorry I was to hear it, and she lightly changed the subject.

"So, it's your turn," she said. "And don't skip the juicy details."

I told her about my growing up the typical tomboy, in love with horses, beating all the neighborhood boys in basketball, infuriated over the injustice of not being able to play football in high school. I admitted that it had never occurred to me that I was a lesbian. "I didn't even know there was such a thing. I was so busy proving I could do everything better than everyone else, I didn't have time to worry about the fact that I was never as interested in boys as all my friends were."

"When did you figure it out?" she asked, her eyes boring into mine.

"I think it was Homecoming night. Believe it or not, I'd been elected Homecoming Queen, and so naturally I had to attend the big dance with Mike Singer, the big man on campus who'd been voted Homecoming King. I was supposed to feel all fluttery or something, but all I could think of was how silly I felt in this long, green dress and high heels. And while we were dancing, with everyone else standing around us like we were some kind of royalty, it occurred to me that I'd much rather be dancing with my best friend, P.J., who was standing there watching us. Unfortunately, what she was longing for was to be in my place, dancing with the Homecoming King."

"Did you ever act on your feelings?"

"Not with P.J. I didn't even let myself think about it. It wasn't until college that I met Martha and a whole new world opened up to me. I went from not even knowing lesbians existed to suddenly seeing them everywhere."

"You and Martha were lovers?"

"Just briefly. It was great while it lasted, but we found ourselves spending more time talking than making love. It was obvious that we made better friends than lovers."

I then told Erica about my long friendship with Martha, my teaching career, and finally I told her about Diane. At some point, my toe brushed against hers, and neither of us moved away. The heat from the spa had sapped all our strength, and our beer bottles were long empty. Still we stayed, hardly able to tear ourselves away from each other.

When she stood up, reaching out to me, I found myself sliding effortlessly into her embrace. It was the most natural feeling in the world. Her lips were impossibly soft, her breasts pressing against mine as we swayed together, locked in a most tender and passionate dance. It took a new burst of rain to send us from the hot tub to my bedroom.

Chapter Nine

Sometimes when the gods smile upon you, it's really just the prelude to a snicker. I had no sooner led Erica to my bedside than the gravelly voice of Sheriff Booker came booming through the window.

"Cassidy? You in there?" The knocking had apparently been going on for some time, but with the jets and bubbles from the hot tub, we hadn't heard a thing. Erica and I raced from the room, scampering into clothes as quickly as we could. By the time I got to the front door, Sheriff Booker and the charming Sergeant Grimes were already inside.

"There you are," the sheriff said. "I was beginning to think something bad had happened to you. Sorry to barge in on you."

"That's okay," I lied. "We were out back and didn't hear you. I take it you got my message."

"Well, actually, no. Sergeant Grimes has been trying to find Ms. Trinidad, and I told him I'd give him an escort out here. She's still here, isn't she?"

Erica came around the corner and said hello to the two men.

"Miss Trinidad, you'll need to come with me." Sergeant Grimes stepped toward her.

"What for?" I asked. "Where to?"

"Now, you just step back and don't cause no problems and everything will be just fine," he said to me. I turned to the sheriff, my eyes pleading for answers.

"Am I under arrest?" Erica asked, incredulous.

"If I need to handcuff you, I will," Grimes said. "If that's the way you want it. If you choose to come on down to the station peaceably, that's fine with me. Either way, I'm bringing you in for questioning."

Sheriff Booker spoke up. "Now, Hank, I don't see any reason to handcuff the lady. She's not exactly resisting arrest. Am I right, Ms. Trinidad?"

Erica stood looking from Booker to Grimes and back again, her bright eyes smoldering.

"It'll be okay, Erica," I said. "I'll call Martha and let her know where you're headed. If you have any problems at all, if anyone so much as puts one finger on you, there'll be hell to pay." I said this looking directly at Grimes, my own anger getting the better of me.

"Sergeant Grimes just wants to question her,

Cass. I'm sure Ms. Trinidad will be back in no time, no worse for the wear. Sometimes these things are better done downtown, that's all."

I stood by and watched helplessly as the fat sergeant herded Erica down the walkway to the rental boat parked behind the sheriff. To her credit, Erica walked ahead of him, and he had to labor to keep up. When they'd pulled away, I turned to the sheriff accusingly.

"Didn't you tell him about the fire? And the boat?" I asked, my voice rising.

"Cass, that stuff doesn't prove anything and you know it. I really don't believe for a second that your friend killed her uncle. But the sergeant there, he's in charge of this investigation, not me. And certainly not you. As it turns out, Ms. Trinidad has been the subject of a murder investigation before, so he's perfectly justified in wanting to question her further. Hopefully, she'll agree to a polygraph and that'll put an end to it. Personally I'd like to see him spend a little more time following other leads."

I heard his words, but my mind had suddenly gone numb. A previous murder investigation? This woman had just spent an hour telling me her life story and hadn't mentioned a word about any such thing! I was beginning to worry that the anger I'd felt for Grimes may have been misplaced.

Sheriff Booker walked me back up to the house, talking the whole while, but my mind refused to hear what he was saying. I caught bits here and there, about the footprints he'd uncovered and his theory about the missing sign. Finally, he stopped and turned to face me.

"Are you listening to a word I'm saying? You look

like you need to sit down." He steered me over to the couch and then went to my refrigerator, bringing back two beers. He opened both, and handed one to me. "Officially, I'm not even supposed to be working today, so one beer can't hurt, can it?" He settled onto the couch opposite me, and took a long drink of his beer. "Tell me what's on your mind, Cass."

"I found out some things today that I want to share with you," I said. "I'm going to tell you anyway, but I'd appreciate it if you'd tell me what you know about Erica being involved in another murder investigation." I'd said it as calmly as I could, but my insides were in turmoil.

"Cass, I swear to you, I don't know any more than I told you. Grimes came barreling into town and damn near busted down my door. The man is not exactly my favorite specimen of a human being, but be that as it may, he's an officer of the law and he wouldn't just make something like that up. But keep in mind, being the subject of a murder investigation does not automatically mean she was guilty of murder. I hope you haven't jumped to that conclusion."

"I haven't, but obviously Grimes has." I took a sip of beer and excused myself long enough to phone Martha. Miraculously, she was still in her office, and I told her of Erica's predicament. Martha told me she'd look into it and not to worry. But I could tell from her tone she was less calm than her words implied.

I returned to the living room and managed to calm myself down enough to tell Booker what I'd found that morning. I told him about Tommy Green admitting to being out on the lake the night of the fire, and about the vandalism at the school. I showed him the green cloth and the cigarette butts and, though I hated to do it, I mentioned that Tommy happened to smoke the same brand. I told him about the frogs and the missing formaldehyde. When I told him why I thought the formaldehyde had been taken, his eyes narrowed but he didn't say a word. I told him about Molly's claim that her sister Mary had been harassed by a boy named Alan Pinkerton who had made a number of crank calls, and I reminded him that Erica herself had received two crank calls. And finally, swearing a silent apology to Lizzie, I told him that Walter Trinidad may have been having an affair with Betty Beechcomb, the postmaster's wife. When at last I'd finished, he sat back and calmly drained his beer.

"You really think someone has Trinidad's privates floating in a jar of formaldehyde?" It was not really a question. "You see, the funny thing is," he said, "when Mrs. Henderson told me about someone lifting their sign, the first thing I thought was that the arsonists might have taken it as a souvenir. There's a lot of weird people in the world, Cass. You figure a few of 'em had to land in Cedar Hills. But now you tell me that the person who took Trinidad's penis might've saved it. Like a souvenir, in a sick kind of way. And the thing is, I just can't see there being two separate souvenir-taking sickos loose at the same time in Cedar Hills. Somehow these cases have to be related. But I'm damned if I know how."

"What do you think the odds would be of two sickos working together?" I asked. "Or more than two."

He thought about that, pulling at his moustache. "You mind if I help myself to another one of your Heinekens? This kind of stuff has a tendency to make me thirsty."

When he came back, he stood at the window, looking out at the pristine lake.

"I only had one case in my life where someone was what I'd call a hundred percent bad. This was back when I was working in Portland, and I caught this guy breaking into a house in the middle of the night. It was pure luck, me catching him at all. The truth was, I was looking for a place to pull over and eat my dinner, and I turned down this residential street and there he was, his rear end disappearing into an upstairs window. Anyway, it turns out this guy was wanted for about twenty different rapes, and what I'd interrupted would've been his next one. Along the way, a few of his victims had had the audacity to fight back, and he'd disfigured them horribly. Not a nice guy. The thing is, even though he was a lone wolf, once he got to prison, he had himself a little following. I think that part bothered me as much as the crimes themselves. The fact that other felons looked up to this guy, emulated the way he walked and talked — that really got to me. Still does. I guess what I'm telling you is, I don't think it's completely beyond the realm of possibility that there could be more than one person committing these crimes. I suppose if there were a couple of bad apples out there, and they found each other, it's possible they could band together." He turned back to the window, rubbing his temples. "This is all pretty wild speculation, you understand. Aside from your little green cloth, and a couple of cigarette butts, we've got diddly squat."

"What about Mrs. Beechcomb?" I asked. "Where do you see her fitting in?"

He stroked his silvery moustache, frowning at me. "Maybe not at all, Cass. Or maybe she hired someone to snuff Trinidad. Or maybe she did it herself. Hell, I don't even know which case I'm working on half the time. One thing's for sure. I'm gonna want to talk to my little buddy, Tommy. And as much as I hate to do it, I'm gonna have to drop in on Mrs. Beechcomb. But I believe I'll start by having a little chat with that Pinkerton boy. As long as Grimes is busy barking up the wrong tree, there's no harm in me checking out some other avenues. I'd like to see who in town has a green jacket with a little hole torn out of it, too."

"What about finding out the blood type from saliva on the cigarette butts? Can't someone do that?" I asked.

"Right now, Cass, those cigarettes don't mean a thing. There's probably no saliva left on them anyway. I believe you're right that the vandals who broke in were the ones who left the butts. And you may be right that they wanted the formaldehyde for the purpose you stated. But unless we can prove that, we've got nothing. I can't exactly ask the D.A.'s office to run an expensive DNA test on a vandalism case. We're going to have to wait until we have more evidence."

The sheriff's beeper went off, and he asked to use my phone. When he came out, his face looked haggard.

"I guess the Pinkerton kid will have to wait," he said. "There's been a boating accident out on Willow Cove. Water skier got run over by his own boat. Can you believe it? It sure does seem that when it rains, it pours."

I walked the sheriff down to his boat.

"Listen, Tom. I think I'll have a chat with the Pinkerton kid myself. Just to get a feel for him. Maybe he'll be less on guard with me than with you, your being the sheriff and all. What do you think?"

He mulled this over while he let his engine warm up. I didn't need his permission and he knew it, but it would be nice to feel we weren't stepping on each other's toes.

After a minute, he nodded his agreement. "But don't show your hand, Cass. Let him think you're looking into the crank calls. See what he was doing the night of the fire. Just be casual, like you're gathering information from all sorts of people. Let him know you're working the Trinidad case too, just as an aside. It might be interesting to see his reaction. Later we can compare notes."

I watched the sheriff's boat pull away, the red and white lights flashing as he sped across the lake. The sky had begun to clear, and it was turning into a very nice afternoon, but my mind was a jumble of confusion. Feelings I hadn't felt in years, maybe ever, had opened up inside me like a fist unclenching. After living so long without allowing myself to feel anything close to passion, I now found myself humming with desire. And just as I was about to let that passion engulf me, I discovered that the object of my desire had not only lied to me but had been the subject of a murder investigation. Not knowing what to think, I preferred not think about it at all.

I decided the best way to get Erica out of my mind was to put myself into action, so I hopped into my Sea Swirl and headed for the county dock.

Chapter Ten

The telephone book listed the Pinkertons on Medley Drive, a few blocks east of the center of town. I routinely passed it on my daily walk through Cedar Hills, and it only took me a few minutes to find the house. I'd decided against calling ahead, figuring the element of surprise was worth the possibility of a wasted trip in the event no one was home. My luck held out. My knock was answered by a middle-aged woman in a yellow and orange shift. Her fleshy cheeks were flushed pink from heat, and I could smell something baking in the kitchen which smelled suspiciously like brownies.

"Mrs. Pinkerton?" I asked.

"Yes?" She held the door open wide while she fanned herself. The smell of brownies was nearly overpowered by the stale sweat that emanated from her.

"I'm Cassidy James, a private investigator. I wonder if I might have a word with your son, Alan." I handed her a business card, which she studied, her eyes narrowing.

"He in some kind of trouble?" she asked. Her glance toward the back of the house told me the boy was home.

"Oh, no. Nothing like that. I'm just looking into several cases that have occurred in town recently, and I'm trying to gather as much information from as many different people as I can. Your son happened to date one of the girls involved in one of the cases, so naturally he's on my list of people who might be able to help us out." I saw in her face she was trying to assimilate this information. She might have been considered a pretty woman, but her eyes had the vague, watery look of someone whose IQ was never going to threaten three digits.

She stepped back from the door and hollered toward the back of the house, "Alan, it's for you!" and then to me, "He'll be out in a minute." Having discharged her motherly duties, she returned to the kitchen, leaving me standing in the doorway. I took this opportunity to ease my way into the living room, which was crowded with overstuffed furniture, a blaring television set and more clutter than I'd ever seen in one room. Diet Coke cans, open potato chip bags and candy bar wrappers littered the surface of nearly every table, and a fat bulldog lay snoring in the corner, oblivious to my presence. I jumped when I heard Alan Pinkerton come up behind me.

"What?" he said, as way of greeting.

My first thought on seeing Alan Pinkerton up close was that this boy was big. Not heavy like his mother, although I could imagine that someday he'd have a gut on him. But this kid was half hormones, half steroids. He wore faded blue Levi's and no shirt, and his hand was tucked just inside the waist of his pants, which he wore low enough on his hips that the darkened trail of hair leading to his genitals was just visible. Jess had said this was a good-looking boy, and on the surface I suppose he was. Tan, blond and muscled, I imagined he ranked right up there with the kind of boys high school girls would find attractive. But his eyes, a surprisingly light blue, were too close together and smallish. His lips were sensuous for a boy, but his mouth seemed mean. And the way he was looking at me, as if he were appraising me sexually, made me immediately uncomfortable.

"You must be Alan," I said, digging in my pocket for a business card. "I'm Cassidy James, a private investigator. I'd like to ask you a few questions. Is there somewhere we could talk?"

"Whatever," he said, a picture of nonchalance. "Come on." He turned and I followed him down a dark hallway to his bedroom. Barbells blocked the doorway, and we stepped over them into a dimly lit room. His shades were drawn, and the walls were covered with heavy metal posters. Not a cheery room, but no sign of severed penises floating in jars either. Alan plopped onto his bed, drawing his knees up under his chin. He seemed incredibly calm, considering the circumstances.

"The reason I wanted to talk to you, Alan, is because I thought you might be able to help me out. You see, last night there was a fire out on Pebble Cove, and a house burned down. Do you know anything about it?"

"No. Why should I?"

"Well, you know how fast news travels in Cedar Hills. I thought maybe you'd heard about it."

"Yeah. So what?"

"Does that mean, yeah you heard about it? Or just yeah, go on."

"I heard about it."

"Okay, good. So you know it was the Hendersons' house that burned down. How does that make you feel?"

His blank stare lasted an eon.

I tried again. "You were close to one of the family members, so I figured you might be upset."

"No," he said. "I couldn't care less." Nice guy. I kept going.

"Well, maybe I didn't get the story straight. I heard that you and Mary were dating. Is that right?"

"I don't see how that's any of your business," he said. Aha. At least the boy could speak in complete sentences. Maybe I was getting somewhere.

"Well, what makes it my business, Alan, is that the Hendersons were receiving threatening phone calls and then their house was burned down, and the police who are pretty good at putting two and two together think there might be a connection."

"Then how come you're here and not them?" he asked. Not as slow as his mother, apparently.

I ignored this question. "How many times did you actually call them before the house burned down?"

"I didn't have nothing to do with that, and no one can say I did. I never threatened nobody, either. So what if I called her up? There's no crime in that, is there?" His tone was threatening, daring me to find fault with his actions.

"Well, you were angry with Mary for not going out with you again. Is that right?"

"That whore?" he said, his voice rising. "No way. Stupid California bitch. I went out with her one time. A total waste of time. What a dog."

Whore? Bitch? Dog? This boy had some anger.

"I thought *she* was the one that wouldn't go out with *you*, Alan. That's why you're so angry with her."

"Oh, yeah, right. Like I care. The only reason I even called her again was to tell her to stop spreading lies about me. I didn't like her uppity attitude either, and I told her so." He began cleaning the unusually long fingernail on his pinky finger with studied boredom.

"So how many times do you think you called her?"

He shrugged, toying with the hair below his navel.

"Just out of curiosity, Alan. Where were you last night? Around ten o'clock?"

He snorted, as if this were the most ridiculous question he could imagine. "I was with friends. You can check it out. We were at Dougie Martin's house.

His parents were home too. Anything else you want to know?"

This threw a whole new light on the matter. If Jess could verify Alan Pinkerton's whereabouts last night, then I was barking up the wrong tree.

"Just a few more questions," I said. "Did you happen to know the man who was killed a few days ago? Walter Trinidad?" The boy's eyes shot up at me, then quickly looked away. An interesting reaction.

"Never even met him."

"Do you smoke?" I asked.

"Sometimes. Why?"

"What brand?"

"Why?" he repeated.

"Just trying to sort things out, Alan. What brand?"

"You got some sort of warrant or something? 'Cause I don't think I have to answer these questions. I don't think whether I smoke or don't smoke is any of your business. I don't think you should even be here. I think you better leave."

"Well, thanks for your help, Alan. I've enjoyed our little chat. If you can think of anything else that might help in these investigations, give me a call. I sure appreciate your assistance."

I could see from the way he was looking at me that I had him confused. Here he'd tried to play tough guy and I was thanking him. He started to push himself off the bed.

"No need to get up, Alan, I can see myself out. And again, thanks for everything."

Mrs. Pinkerton had lodged herself in an easy chair, a plate of brownies before her, and was so engrossed in the TV that she didn't hear me leave. Outside, I gulped the fresh air, grateful to be out of the dark, overly warm house. Alan Pinkerton may not have had anything to do with Walter Trinidad's murder or the Hendersons' fire, but he acted guilty of something. I could hardly wait to hear Sheriff Booker's impression of him. My own gut was screaming "Bad Apple, Bad Apple, Bad Apple!" But then, like old Jake used to tell me, you can't always rely on first impressions.

Chapter Eleven

The postmaster's house sat high on a bluff overlooking the lake, not far from the Pinkertons' house, and since I was almost in the neighborhood, I thought I'd drop by for a visit. I was hoping that Ed spent his Saturdays out on the lake rather than in front of the television. I wanted the chance to chat with Betty Beechcomb alone. To my relief, his car was not in the driveway.

She greeted me at the door wearing a shimmering, sheer halter top, bright pink Danskin tights and her ever-present high heels. A strange getup for anywhere, let alone at home alone. I wondered if she was expecting someone else. I introduced myself and she waved me in cheerily, retrieving a half-empty glass with what looked like gin or vodka from the counter on her way into the living room. A Donna Summer tune blared from two large speakers, and she sort of danced her way over to the stereo to turn down the volume. From the scuffed indentations in the recently vacuumed carpet, I gathered she'd been dancing when I arrived.

"Mrs. Beechcomb," I started, "I'm working on a case involving the murder of Walter Trinidad, and I understand that you were, uh, friends with him." No point in beating around the bush, I thought.

Her heavily made up eyes grew wide for a fraction of a second, and then she threw back her head and laughed. Her bleached blond hair was pulled up into a ponytail, which bobbed on the top of her head. When she'd quit laughing, she took a long swig of her drink, rattling the cubes around. "I suppose in a town this small, it was bound to come out sooner or later," she said, studying her lacquered red nails.

"Forgive me," I said, "but you don't seem too upset."

"Oh?" She appraised me coolly. "Did you know Walter well?"

"No," I admitted, wondering how she'd managed to turn this around.

"Well, I did. He was a tedious bore. And a terrible lover, I might add. He had the teensiest little pecker you ever saw. Not that a pecker is everything. But it should at least be there, shouldn't it?"

Not necessarily, I thought wryly. But this wasn't

the time to wax philosophical about the male appendage. "Then why, may I ask, did you go out with him?"

"Because I was bored! B-O-R-E-D, bored! God, what a tiny, tacky town this is. Don't you ever get bored, dear? Well, no. I suppose not." She eyed me disdainfully.

"Can you tell me where you were on Wednesday evening?" I asked, watching her closely.

"Out. O-U-T, as in out on the town. Wednesday is Ed's bowling night. I pretend to begrudge him his few nights out. Ha! I practically live for Wednesdays."

I was beginning to fear that if she insisted on spelling everything, I'd still be there when Ed returned. This was not a conversation I wanted to have in his presence. "Can you tell me where you went? And with whom?"

"I'd rather not." She plucked an ice cube from her glass and sucked noisily. "Oh, all right." She sighed, letting the cube fall from her lips back into the glass. "What possible difference can it make? I was with a boy. A local boy. Perhaps you know him. Quite a young stallion, if you know what I mean. Name of Tommy Green." I'm afraid my jaw must have dropped, because she graced me with another one of her laughs. "I see you do know Tommy. Perhaps you've been out with him too?"

"Uh, no," I stammered. I felt my cheeks turn embarrassingly hot at the suggestion. "Where did you two go?" I asked, trying to regain control of the conversation.

"Oh, just out in his darling little speedboat. Tommy has some marvelous grass. We smoked a little, drank some gin, you know."

"What time did you get back?"

"Before eleven. Ed gets home around then and I wanted to be in bed before he got here."

"And did Tommy know you were also seeing Trinidad?" I asked. Her eyes narrowed and she got up to fix herself another drink, talking over her shoulder. I followed her into the kitchen and couldn't help noticing the large butcher knife lodged into the wood block holder on the counter.

"I didn't think anyone knew about Walter. It's certainly not something I was going to discuss with another man. Frankly, I don't even know how you found out."

But I had found out. And maybe Tommy had too. And maybe little Tommy did not take kindly to another man messing with his woman. I shook from my head the grisly image of Tommy slicing away at Trinidad. "And how about Friday night? Were you with Tommy then too?"

"My, you do get around. As a matter of fact I was. Ed had an Elks Lodge meeting. Those always turn into late nights at that dreadful little tavern, so I knew I had until midnight and I made the most of it."

"What did you think of the fire?" I asked. "I bet that took you by surprise." She fell for the bluff easily.

"Wasn't that something!" she said, her dark eyes widening. "Tommy, of course, wanted to rush over there and help, but I convinced him that we couldn't very well be seen pulling up to the dock together. Besides, we were too stoned to be much help to anyone. But I think he was a little peeved at me over that." So Tommy had lied about seeing the fire. I wondered what else he might have lied about.

"Do you smoke, Mrs. Beechcomb?"

"You mean cigarettes? Oh, just now and then. Whenever I'm with someone else who smokes. I don't actually ever buy cigarettes. I just mooch them. I suppose you think that's awful."

Here was a woman who admitted to cheating on her husband, apparently as a matter of course, who refused to help with a burning house, and she thought I'd think less of her for mooching cigarettes.

"Did you know the Hendersons?" I asked, changing gears.

"Are you suggesting I had something to do with that fire?" she asked, fanning herself as if the room had suddenly grown terribly warm. In fact it was quite cool where I was standing.

"I just wondered if you knew them."

"Him, you mean. You wondered if I knew him! Well, of course I do, and obviously you already know that, or you wouldn't be asking. But I did not have an affair with Bob Henderson. For your information, he was not very, shall we say, responsive, to my advances. I'm not a thin-skinned woman. I know how to handle rejection."

I suddenly wondered if somehow Trinidad had rejected her, and if her way of handling that rejection involved a butcher knife.

Outside, the crunch of gravel told us Ed Beechcomb had arrived home early. Startled, she looked up, and for the first time, she seemed somewhat rattled.

"I'd appreciate your not blabbing any of this," she

said, hurriedly ushering me to the door. "I understand you have to ask your little questions and I've tried to be patient and answer things that are none of your business. And you must know I've been totally honest, even though I know my improprieties must seem shocking to someone like you. I haven't lied about anything," she said, practically shoving me out the door.

But she had, I mused, smiling at her. I'd seen a carton of Virginia Slims on the top of the refrigerator, and for some reason I didn't think Ed Beechcomb was the type to smoke them.

"Thanks so much!" she shouted gaily, waving good-bye. "And if you get any more of those little lip gloss tubes in, let me know!" Apparently she wanted Ed to think I was the Avon lady.

I left, smiling briefly at Ed, who barely looked up, his face so long and drawn I was afraid that the news of Betty's infidelities had finally reached the post office.

Chapter Twelve

It was nearly six when I got back to my house, and Martha's boat, which she kept at the marina, was tied up to my dock. I hurried up to see what she'd found out about Erica, and when I walked in, the two of them were lounging in the living room, shoes kicked off, drinking wine. Erica was doing a pretty good imitation of Sergeant Grimes.

"There you are," Martha said. "I thought you'd be slaving over a hot stove!" She got up to hug me, something we automatically did on greeting, and over her shoulder I saw Erica watching us with interest.

"I was out detecting," I said, getting a wineglass. "How did it go with Grimes?" I still hadn't looked Erica in the eye. I hadn't had time to sort out my feelings, and I didn't quite know how to act.

"He wanted me to take a lie detector test," Erica said. "He said if I was innocent, I had nothing to fear, and that if I refused, he could book me on suspicion of murder and do it the hard way. The guy's obviously been watching too many Clint Eastwood movies. Anyway, I agreed."

Martha was sitting in my favorite chair, so I sat down on the sofa, leaving a lot of space between Erica and myself. Panic and Gammon were already entrenched on her lap, purring happily.

"So how did it go?" I asked.

"Do you mean did I pass?" Erica asked. "Don't tell me you're starting to have your doubts too?"

"I didn't mean that at all," I lied. "It's just that there were things you seem to have left out of your story. Such as being the subject of an earlier murder investigation, for example. I just wonder what else you haven't told me."

"Oh, I see," Erica said sarcastically. "So you do think maybe I killed my uncle. This is great."

"I'm sure that's not what Cass meant, Erica," Martha said, playing peacemaker. "Is it, Cassie?" She raised an eyebrow at me. This was Martha's way of telling me to cool it, but I was already angry.

"You left out a pretty important detail, especially considering that you hired me knowing you were a suspect in this case. It's not like this was some insignificant little episode. I mean, come on Erica. What was I supposed to think? Better yet, what were you thinking?"

Erica got up, dumping both cats from her lap. She stormed into the kitchen, and turned back, her eyes livid. "I guess I didn't want to break the mood by bringing up something I'd rather forget. I guess I thought that you trusted me enough that when you did hear about it, you wouldn't just automatically jump to the conclusion that I was guilty. I hoped you thought more highly of me than that. And I guess I was wrong." She stormed out, leaving Martha and me staring after her.

"Nice going, champ," Martha said. "You want to go apologize now, or you want to hear the story?"

"I don't know what I want," I said miserably.

"Well, listen up. First off, she passed the polygraph with flying colors. I talked to Mike Wong who sat in with Grimes while he interrogated her. He got pretty rough, from what I hear. A couple of times Wong had to intervene. Anyway, just over a year ago, Erica *was* involved in a murder case, but no charges were ever brought against her. In fact, if anything, she turned out to be something of a hero. Unfortunately, she was too late to save her lover."

"What do you mean?" I asked, beginning to feel sick to my stomach.

"Erica was working on a book. Did you know she's a writer? Anyway, she was in her study working and it was way past midnight when she heard her lover, Anne, screaming from the upstairs bedroom. She went charging up there and burst into the bedroom. There was this guy, a nylon stocking over his head, choking the shit out of her. He'd been in the process of raping her and when she tried to fight back, he started choking her. Erica grabbed the first thing she could find, which turned out to be a golf club leaning against the wall. She started hitting the guy over the head and back, all the while he was choking Anne. Erica was yelling at him to stop, to get off, but he just kept on choking her until finally he fell to the floor. She said he never even tried to fight her off. He was so intent on killing Anne that he didn't even try to defend himself. By the time Erica could reach her, she was already dead. Erica tried CPR, but it was too late. Apparently the whole thing only took a few minutes. Just like that, both her lover and the man who killed her were dead. Her whole life fell apart."

I sat there numbly. No wonder she hadn't wanted to talk about it. What a jerk I was. Martha saw the look on my face and came over to sit beside me. She put her arm around me, pulling me close.

"There's no way you could have known, Cass, so don't beat yourself. Anyway, Grimes, true to form, tried to insinuate that Erica, being a man-hating dyke who'd already killed a man once for rape, had done the same to her uncle when he tried to get a little too intimate with her. He talked to all sorts of people in town who claimed that Trinidad was acting like Erica was more than his niece. He ran a check on her, and when the computer turned up her part in the previous case, he went ape-shit. He was positive she'd flunk the polygraph and that he'd get her to confess. But Wong says she did real good. Even Grimes is admitting now that she may be innocent. Although he still doesn't want her leaving town. Polygraphs aren't foolproof, after all."

"I can't believe I said that to her."

"Hey. So you stuck your foot in your mouth. Go apologize. I'll wait here." Martha gave me a little

120

shove, and I got off the couch, making the long trek down the hall to the guest room. Her door was shut and I knocked. Receiving no answer, I opened the door and peeked in. Erica was throwing clothes into her overnight bag with barely contained fury.

"Erica?" I said. "Can I come in?"

"Suit yourself."

I walked over and sat on the end of the bed. "Sometimes, I'm an asshole."

"Obviously." She wasn't going to make this any easier.

"It's just that I felt like you weren't being up front with me. Like you didn't trust me enough to confide in me. When the sheriff told me you'd been involved in a murder case, I didn't know what to think. All I knew is that you'd lied to me, and that hurt."

"I never lied to you." She turned to face me. Her eyes were the color of sapphires, and they burned right through me.

"By omission," I said. "You lied by omission."

"I'm sure there were a few things you skipped right over yourself," she said. "Anyway, I didn't exactly feel like going into it right then. And I really don't feel like going into it again right now either. If it's all the same to you, I think I'd feel more comfortable over at the lodge tonight. I'm sure Martha will give me a ride."

"I'm sure she will," I said. It wasn't all the same to me at all, but I'd be damned if I'd say so.

"Maybe we can do the dinner another time," she said, walking past me, her overnight bag slung over her shoulder.

"Yeah, sure." I stayed sitting on the edge of the

bed, doing my best not to break into tears. I didn't know if I was more angry or hurt. All I knew was, Erica was leaving and I didn't want her to. But I'd apologized enough. I wasn't going to grovel.

Martha tapped on the door and pushed it open. "I guess that didn't go too great, huh?" she said. "You gonna be okay?"

I nodded and waved her away.

"You want me to come back over after I drop her off? You still want to talk about the case?"

I shook my head no and again waved her away.

"If you want to talk, call me," she said, backing out the door. I listened to them leave, but stayed on the bed long after the whine of Martha's boat had faded, alone with my conflicting emotions.

Chapter Thirteen

My dreams that night were fitful. Several times I awoke bathed in sweat, with images of severed penises and burning houses swirling in my head. But the last dream I had made up for all the others. It started in a hot tub, moved into the bedroom and was not interrupted by knocking on the door. My heart was still pounding wildly when I got out of bed Sunday morning.

After my shower, which I admit was less hot than usual, I dressed in jeans and a white button-down blouse that Martha always said showed off my tan.

The day outside promised to be sunny, and both Gammon and Panic were anxious to go for a romp in the woods. It had been days since they'd been outside, and as I fed them, I promised them that when I returned we'd all go outside together. This seemed to satisfy them, and they curled up in a patch of sun on the sofa.

Over coffee and toast, I planned my next course of action. Regardless of Erica's feelings for me, I intended to go through with the investigation. For one thing, this was my first real case, and I felt a strong need to succeed. Even if it turned out to be my last, I wanted to be able to hold my head up in town. By now, the way news traveled in Cedar Hills, I figured half the town knew I was a private investigator. For better or worse, my identity had changed. I'd rather be known as the one who caught the "Cedar Hills Killer," as the locals dubbed Trinidad's murderer, than the one who had tried and failed. For another thing, I was totally hooked, and felt a personal desire to catch the killer. I admitted that I also wanted to impress Erica.

The first thing I needed to do was to confirm Alan Pinkerton's claim that he'd spent the night with Jess's son, and that Jess could vouch for his presence there around ten o'clock. It would be nice to be able to rule somebody out. And, I decided, while I was out and about, I'd keep my eyes open for someone with a torn jacket. I'd started doubting my own theory about why someone had broken into the science room, even though I'd managed to convince Booker that it was at least a possibility.

It was getting harder and harder to connect Trinidad's murder with the other crimes in town, but it would be foolish not to follow up on the few clues I had. It was obvious that Tommy wasn't the only one in town who smoked Marlboros. The fact that Tommy had lied about seeing the fire didn't bother me as much as the fact that on both the night of the murder and the night of the arson, he was out in his boat on the lake, without running lights, supposedly with a woman who had either slept with or come on to both of the victims. Had they done it together? I wondered. If so, what was the motive? Revenge for rejection? Jealousy? And then there was Ed Beechcomb. Could he really be so blind as not to notice that his wife was sleeping with every male in town? I made a note to check on Ed's attendance at Wednesday night's bowling and Friday's Elks Lodge meeting. Suddenly, I had a busy day ahead of me.

I said good-bye to my furry companions, admonishing Panic not to let her portly sister eat all the crunchies in their bowl, and went out into what was shaping up to be a glorious day. The sun had already warmed the morning air, and mist rose from the water in vaporous puffs which floated lazily upward before disappearing into the bright blue sky. Blue heron cruised the shore while ospreys took turns diving into the water, fishing for bluegill and sunfish along the surface. The Sunday water skiers had not yet ventured out on the lake, so the only sounds were the exultant cries of the birds and the thunderous splashes when they dove.

For a moment, I considered scrapping my plans, setting up a chair on the dock and trying out my new fly rod. But a sense of determination urged me full speed across the glassy lake. Sometimes the sheer pleasure of ripping along at a fast clip, hair blowing straight back, being sprayed by water, is as much as a person can hope for. By the time I arrived at the marina, I was in much better spirits.

Buddy Drake was at the gas dock with Tommy when I arrived, and he waved me over. I noticed his usually scraggly black moustache had been neatly trimmed and his hair was slicked back with some kind of gel, making him look quite dapper. I'd hardly ever seen him without his baseball cap, and I wondered idly if Buddy might not have a romantic interest somewhere along his mail route. Smiling, I wondered if he knew Betty Beechcomb. He greeted me with a huge grin. "I hear you were quite the hero the other night. Congratulations."

"You've been listening to Jess Martin too much," I said, laughing.

"Actually, it was Sheriff Booker that mentioned it. He seems quite taken with you. Too bad he's already married, huh?" Buddy had been trying to set me up with various locals for three years. I think he knew my preferences leaned toward women, but he was on a mission to save me. "You think your pal wants her uncle's mail, or should I have it held at the post office?" He ran his hand over his slicked back hair.

"I guess you better have it held," I said. "I don't think she's going to be staying in town very long." The realization that this was probably true hit me unexpectedly. But I couldn't allow myself to dwell on it. I had a case to solve.

"Yeah, from what I hear, the cops are startin' to look elsewhere. I guess she's been cleared, eh?"

I was always amazed at the speed with which news traveled in this town. My own guess was that Buddy himself was largely responsible for this. His boat route took him from dock to dock, where more often than not people rushed out to greet him. What he learned from one person, he passed on to the next. By the time he was done with his morning route, he knew everything there was to know, and so did everyone else.

"You got any leads yet? This thing has got people all riled up. Some think the fire out at the Hendersons might be a related incident. Any truth to that notion?"

I knew I was being pumped for information, but I figured I could put Buddy's gossiping skills to good use. If the killer thought the police were closing in on him, maybe he'd do something dumb to tip his hand. So I lied, big time.

"Well, this is just between you and me," I lowered my voice, "but I think we're closing in on 'em. Things are really starting to fall into place now. I really can't say more than that, though, or the sheriff will have my hide."

"Yeah, that's pretty much what he told me, too," he said, lying smoothly. Unless, of course, Tom Booker was as devious as I was and had planted the same information with Buddy. Either way, I felt confident that it would be no time at all before the murderer, whoever he or she was, heard that an arrest was imminent.

Buddy wished me good luck and Tommy told me to be careful. I eyed him, wondering if there was some hidden meaning in his warning, but he smiled innocently, his elfin face as carefree as a cherub's. Which I knew didn't mean a thing.

I tossed the kitchen trash bag I'd brought into the rusty dumpster and headed to Jess Martin's. One of these days, I'd have to start my car, I mused, passing my Jeep Cherokee in its usual spot, next to the dumpster. The last thing I needed was a dead battery. With a pang of regret, I noticed Erica's red Miata was no longer parked at the marina.

Jess's house was right on Main Street, a block from Loggers Tavern. One of the benefits of living in a tiny town was that people didn't have to worry too much about drunk driving. All three bars were within easy walking distance from most homes. I could see Jess's legs sticking out from under an old gray Chevy parked in front, and as I got nearer, I could hear him humming to himself.

"Haven't you got that bucket of bolts running yet?" I said. His feet jerked, and I heard a loud thump, followed by a curse. "Oops, sorry. Didn't mean to startle you," I said sheepishly.

Jess pushed himself out from under the wreck and sat up, rubbing his head. His brown hair had been recently washed and his ponytail was still a little damp, but the stubble of beard on his lean cheeks showed, as always, at least two days' worth of growth. I wondered how he managed to keep it at that exact length without ever actually growing a beard.

"Oh, that's okay," he said. "Might've knocked some sense into me."

"Jess, there's something I want to ask you. I was talking to Alan Pinkerton yesterday, and he said that on Friday he and some other boys spent the night at your house."

Jess looked at me curiously, then stood up and leaned against the car. "That's right, Cass, he did. Dougie had a couple of friends over that night.

Bonnie fixed up the bunk room this summer and they usually stay out there. I think they rented some dirty movies, to tell you the truth. Every time I went to the back part of the house, they were laughing and making lewd noises. And I suspect they were drinking beer too. I guess our philosophy on that is, we'd rather have them doing that kind of stuff at home than out driving around where they could get into some real trouble. Why all this sudden interest in Pinkerton?"

"Jess, I know you eat lunch with Buddy Drake, and I know you two gossip like crazy. But if I ask you to not tell him or anyone else something, can I count on you?"

"Cassie, you have my word on it," he said without hesitation. I knew he meant it.

"I have a bad feeling about that kid — Pinkerton. I know he's your son's friend and all, but personally he gives me the creeps. Anyway, there's a slight possibility that he might have had something to do with the fire out at the Hendersons'. Erica and I saw a boat leaving the scene, with no running lights. I know that there were other boats out there without lights around that time, but Pinkerton had been calling the older Henderson girl, harassing her for not going out with him. I don't have any actual proof, you understand, but instinct tells me that he might be involved. Except if you can say with certainty that he was at your house around ten, then I can cross him off the list."

Jess reached into his shirt pocket and took out one of his hand-rolled cigarettes. He lit it, took a deep drag and exhaled, blowing crooked smoke rings skyward. "The thing is, Cass," he said, finally, "I can't really say for sure where he was at ten o'clock. I mean, the boys came over around six. They were in and out, tossing a football in the back yard, listening to Doug's cassettes, watching dirty movies and who knows what else. I know they ordered a pizza from Kings Harbor around seven-thirty because the delivery boy came to the front door and I showed him how to get to the back. But hell, me and Bonnie were in bed by nine. She gets up at five and likes her eight hours of sleep. I suppose it's possible someone could have slipped away without us even knowing. I do know they must've stayed up late, because they were all sleepin' in the next morning. But that's usual. Whenever they get together for a sleepover they tend to stay up half the night. I guess I'm not bein' much help here, am I?"

"Do they have these sleepovers often?" I asked.

"During the summer they do lots. Sometimes our house, sometimes over at one of the other boys'. A couple of times a week, I'd say."

"Who all did Doug have over that night?"

"Oh, just his usual buddies. Dunk Foster — he's that tall kid that bags groceries at McGregors — and Pinkerton. Those three are always together. Have been since about ninth grade. I've been after Dougie to get some new friends, on account of these guys are always ditching school and such, but Bonnie says we gotta let the boy find his own way, make his own decisions. Do you really think they might've started that fire, Cass?" Jess's eyes searched mine, worry clouding his face.

"I hope not, Jess. Arson is a serious charge, and even though they're not eighteen, they could be tried as adults. At least no one was hurt in the fire. It could have been worse. But if they did do it, there's a chance they might be involved in other things too."

I could see Jess thinking this through. He pinched out his cigarette with his forefinger and thumb, having wetted them first with his tongue. How he avoided burning himself, I didn't know, but I'd seen him do this often enough that I'd quit worrying. He put the remaining stub in his shirt pocket. Later he'd mix the unused tobacco with other stubs and roll himself a new cigarette.

"If you're right about this, and Dougie was involved in that fire, I won't stand in your way. I hope to God you're wrong. I mean, the boy is a royal pain in the ass sometimes, but he's still just a kid. I just hope you're wrong."

"So do I, Jess." I wondered if I should tell him about the incident in McGregors, but Jess had enough on his mind at the moment. "Tell me something. Where was little Jess when the boys had their sleepover?"

"Oh, she was at home. She wants like crazy to be accepted by Dougie and his friends, but they won't give her the time of day. I know she went back there to see if they'd give her a piece of pizza, even though I told her to just leave them alone, and sure enough she came back empty-handed with her feelings all hurt. She went to bed about the same time we did. If you're thinking Jessie had anything to do with it, you're nuts. That kid's good as gold."

"I know that, Jess. I'm just thinking she might be able to tell me more. Like maybe she knows for sure they were there around ten because she heard them laughing and it woke her up. Something like that. It would be nice if we could substantiate their being there."

"Well, you're welcome to talk to her, if you want. She's inside cleaning her room. She's got a mowing job in about an hour, so you're lucky you came by early. But, Cass, try not to let on that you suspect those boys of causing that fire. I'd just as soon that rumor not get started. I mean, if it turns out that's what happened, I'll support the police all the way. But I'd hate to see my son's reputation ruined because of a rumor that turns out not to be true."

"Word of honor," I said, holding up three fingers in the Girl Scout salute.

"Let me know what you find out. You know I'm going to worry about this now until you do."

I reached up and gave Jess a hug which he returned somewhat awkwardly before breaking free to disappear under his car again. I left him to his mechanics, and let myself in through the screen door.

"Jessie?" I called. Receiving no answer, I made my way to the back of the house, peeking in open doors as I went. I was glad Bonnie was at work. It gave me a chance to snoop around a little. It was easy to spot Doug's room, with its unmade bed, crumpled clothes and Metallica posters on the wall. Just like Alan Pinkerton's, I thought. But being a slob and having bad taste in music were not a crime. Hoping that Doug wouldn't materialize from somewhere down the hall, I stepped into his room for a better look. I noticed a green nylon jacket among the heap of clothing piled on the bed. Heart racing, I inched forward and lifted the jacket, examining it closely in the dim light coming from the hallway.

132

There were no holes or tears to be seen. But the color and feel of the fabric were perfect. And with growing excitement, I noticed a huge orange logo across the back. Cedar Hills Ducks. This was a team jacket. Which meant there were more of these out there. And one of them had a tear in it. I'd have given anything to go through Pinkerton's closet. Or maybe Dunk's. Pretty soon, that torn jacket was bound to turn up. These thoughts were interrupted by a voice behind me.

"Looking for something?" I jumped about a foot and threw the jacket back onto the bed. When I turned around, little Jess was grinning at me, her braces gleaming in the hall light.

"Shoot, Jessie, you scared the daylights out of me. How you doin'?"

"I'm fine, Miss James. You looking for Dougie? He's not here."

"Actually, kiddo, it's you I wanted to see. Your dad said you were cleaning your room. Obviously this one isn't yours."

She giggled at this, wrinkling her nose at the general filth in her brother's room.

"Mine's down here. Come on. I'll show you."

I followed her into a brightly lit room painted yellow, with pictures of airplanes and rockets adorning the walls. The room wasn't spotless by any standards, but it was neat and cheerful and lacked the gloom and raunchiness of her brother's.

"You like aviation, I see," I said, settling on the edge of her bed.

"Yeah. I used to want to be a pilot. Or maybe even an astronaut. But now I'm thinking of going into something else." Her eyes shone with excitement, and I noticed with a pang that she stood with the exact same stance, using the exact same mannerisms as her dad.

"Oh yeah? Like what?"

"Promise you won't laugh?" she said seriously.

"Cross my heart and hope to die."

"I'm thinking about going into law enforcement."

"That's great, Jessie. You mean like a cop?"

"Or maybe the FBI or CIA. I haven't decided for sure. I could even be a detective like you."

"Well, I think that's great. You'd make a very good law enforcement officer. You know what you ought to do? You ought to ask my friend Martha if some day she'd let you make the rounds with her. That would give you a firsthand taste of what being a cop is like."

Her green eyes widened behind the wire-frame glasses, making her look like a cute little owl. "You think she'd let me?"

"I could put in a good word for you, if you want. I think she could be talked into it." I knew I'd owe Martha something really gourmet for this one.

"That'd be neat," she said. "So, how come you wanted to see me?" She jumped up onto the edge of the dresser, her red tennies swinging freely off the floor.

"I wanted to ask you about the other night when Doug had some friends over. Night before last. Remember?"

"Oh sure. The Three Musketeers. They slept out in the bunk room." She pointed out the window where what had once been a detached garage now sported a fresh coat of blue paint, with drapes hanging in the windows. Bonnie had made a nice little addition to the house.

"Do they call themselves that?"

"No way. That's just what Dad and I call them behind their backs." She tucked a loose strand of long brown hair behind her ear. I'd seen Jess do the same a hundred times.

"Do you know what they did that night, Jessie? Your dad said you might know more than he does."

"They wouldn't even let me in," she said. "They used to, but not anymore. I know for sure they rented an X-rated movie, because I saw it on Dougie's dresser. And they were drinking too. Alan Stinkerton always brings over a bunch of liquor. They sit around smoking and drinking and talking dirty. They think they're big shots because they're seniors and everything."

I smiled. "What kind of cigarettes does Dougie smoke?" I asked, thinking "Stinkerton" was perfect.

"He used to steal Dad's tobacco and roll his own. But now he's strictly a Marlboro Man. That's how he says it too — 'I'm strictly a Marlboro Man.' It's pretty funny, actually." A coincidence? I wondered.

"It sounds like you and your brother don't always see eye to eye," I said. "Like yesterday in the store," I added, watching her carefully.

She looked away. "He's a jerk. I know that sounds bad to say about your own brother, but I'm just telling the truth. It's funny, 'cause I used to look up to him, you know? But not anymore. I think he's just plain mean." I decided not to pursue the store incident. She was clearly embarrassed by my having seen her humiliated in public.

"Do you know if he and his friends went out the other night, or if they stayed in the bunk house the whole time?" I asked, getting back to the main point.

"Why?"

"I'm just trying to establish where they were about ten o'clock that night. I thought maybe you'd know, seeing as how your window looks right out there. Maybe you heard them or saw them. Can you say for sure that they were home at that time?"

"Well, not for absolute sure." She seemed to be stalling for time, deciding how much she should tell me.

"Jessie, this is important. You need to level with me."

"Is Dougie in trouble? He'd kill me if I ratted on him."

"To be honest, I don't know. But I need to know the truth so I can help him if I can. Did you see them leave that night?"

"Not exactly. Actually, I know they were there when I went to bed, because the TV was still on. They were still watching that movie. I fell asleep and I didn't hear anything again until about two in the morning — I know because I looked at my clock. The reason I woke up is because they were arguing. I heard the bunk house door slam, and I got up and looked out. The lights were on and I could see them through the window. I couldn't hear what they were saying, but it looked like Dougie was really ticked off at Alan. Dunk had to break them up because they were that close to fighting."

"If you had to guess what they were fighting about, what would be your best guess?"

Jessie bit her lip, thinking hard. "Well, Dougie

mad, which means Stinkerton probably did something stupid that could get them in trouble. Like the time he talked Dunk into stealing a case. of Budweiser from McGregors and almost got Dunk fired. Dunk had to work without pay to make up for it, and now they watch him like a hawk. Or the time he wrote Dougie's initials on a stop sign they'd marked up with those stupid swastikas. They never got busted for that, but Dougie was really ticked off."

The mention of swastikas caused my pulse to hammer. "Any idea where they might've been until two in the morning?"

Jessie paused long enough that I knew she was withholding something. "Not really," she said, looking down at her swinging tennis shoes.

"Come on, Jessie. I need your help."

"I really don't know for sure."

"But you have an idea, right?" I asked, secretly crossing my fingers.

"Well." She paused, biting her lip. "Sometimes they sneak out and go to their fort. No one's supposed to know about it. Please don't ask Doug about it, okay? He'll kill me for real. And don't tell Dad."

"How come you know about the fort, if no one's supposed to know?"

"Because I followed them one time," she said, her big eyes gleaming mischievously.

"Weren't you afraid they'd catch you?"

"Kinda." She nodded. "I stayed way back, especially when they went through the train tunnel. That was the scariest part because a train can come right through and there's hardly any space between the wall and the train. Luckily, none came, but I had to wait until they got through the tunnel before I could go through, otherwise all they had to do was look back and they'd have seen me. It took me a while to figure out which way they'd gone."

"And where did they go, Jessie? Where is this fort of theirs?"

"It's only about a mile from here, but it's in this old logging site, and it's totally private. You can't tell there's anything even there until you get up close. It's pretty cool. They've got a boom box out there. They turned it up real loud, which is partly how I figured which way they went. I was afraid to get too close, though, so I didn't get to see inside."

"Could you find it again?" I asked. "Could you take me to it?"

"Maybe." She sounded unsure. "But I can't, honest. You don't know my brother. I have to live with him. If he knew I took you there, I'd be dead. You gotta believe me." There was serious fear in her eyes, and I wondered just how real the threat was.

"Okay, Jessie. Tell you what. Let's compromise. Draw me a map. I promise not to tell anyone how I found my way to the fort, and hopefully no one will even know I was ever there. I just want to get a look at it. I won't touch a thing, honest."

Jess looked up, her bright eyes calculating rapidly. "You tell me what Dougie did to get in trouble, and I'll draw you the map," she said. Maybe the little booger ought to forget about law enforcement and go into negotiating, I thought.

"I promised your dad I wouldn't tell anyone," I said. "It's not that he doesn't trust you, but he's trying to be fair to Doug. See, Doug probably hasn't done anything wrong. I'm just trying to find out who did. Okay?"

Jessie shook her head, obviously frustrated. "It's not fair. Dad's always trying to protect him. He always lets him get away with everything. Dougie never does anything good, and he's the one that gets all the privileges. I do everything right, and I'm the one stuck with always cleaning up Doug's messes. I hate him!" She jumped off the dresser and fumbled around in a drawer, coming up with a pencil and sheet of paper. Silently, she sat at her tiny desk and painstakingly drew a detailed map to the fort. It took a full five minutes, with a few erasures, but the final product was a work of art.

"I owe you one, sport," I said, offering a handshake which she returned hesitantly.

"And just for the record, I have a feeling your dad thinks you are pretty special. He's so proud of you he can hardly contain himself. It could be he tries to bend over backward for Dougie so as not to seem partial to you. You understand what I'm telling you?"

She looked down, slightly embarrassed, but obviously pleased. "I guess so," she said, playing with her ponytail. "I just get mad sometimes. I wish Dougie would just be nicer, is all. We used to have fun when I was little. But that was a long time ago. I keep wishing he'd change back to how he used to be, but I don't think he's going to. You know? I mean, I think I finally realized that he's not going to get any nicer. I might as well accept it, I guess."

"You just wait. He may just be going through a phase. Sometimes people do become more considerate as they get older." I wished I could say something more encouraging, but from what I'd seen of Dougie myself, I didn't hold out much hope for him becoming a wonderful human being in the near future.

I thanked Jessie for the help and promised once again not to tell anyone about the existence of the fort. I wasn't sure what I hoped to learn by traipsing out into the woods looking for some boys' hideout, but my natural nosiness made it impossible for me to ignore, despite the fact that I was beginning to feel I was chasing false leads. Even if I tracked down every Marlboro smoker in Cedar Hills, I still wouldn't be one step closer to solving Trinidad's murder, or even the Hendersons' fire. And just because Pinkerton and his little group of buddies were self-styled neo-Nazis didn't mean they had anything to do with either crime. But like my old mentor Jake Parcell used to say, you can't rule someone out until you can rule 'em out. A brilliant man, Jake. So I tucked my increasing doubts about my detective skills far back in my head, where I could almost ignore them, and set out to do some good, old-fashioned rule-outs.

Chapter Fourteen

Since McGregors was just down the street, I decided to have a word with Dunk, the bag boy. As soon as I saw him, I realized I'd seen him a hundred times before. He was gangly and tall, with a pimply complexion, crooked teeth and flaming red hair shaved into a crew cut. He stooped, like so many tall people do, his narrow shoulders hunched forward like wounded wings. It was hard to picture this boy ever doing anything remotely athletic, but then again, Jess had said the team was hard up for players. Even so, I doubted Dunk had the competitive drive or energy to want to play. My guess was, he had an athletic father who was reliving his old fantasies through Dunk. Dunk looked like he'd rather be back in bed.

I watched him for a few minutes, while he bagged a lady's groceries as if he were underwater. Slow, listless and bored. I doubted he got many tips. When she was gone, I walked up to Eileen, the grocery clerk, and asked her if she minded my borrowing her bag boy for a few minutes. Eileen was a large woman with whom I'd had many friendly exchanges over the years. I liked her, and she always made a point of telling me what the specials were. I think she worried that I wasn't eating enough, because now and then she'd throw in these cellophane-wrapped pie slices the Women's Elks Club made for fundraisers, and she'd wink and refuse to take my money.

"Well," Eileen said, looking around the nearly empty store, "I don't know what anyone would want with him, as much use as he's been lately, but you're welcome to him."

I chuckled, but Dunk narrowed his eyes at her, obviously not taking the good-natured insult with humor. He looked like a boy long accustomed to insult, finding it even when it wasn't there.

"Dunk," I said, handing him a business card and lowering my voice, "my name is Cassidy James and I wondered if you'd mind stepping out back with me for a few minutes to answer some questions."

"Go on back by the dumpsters," Eileen told me. "That's real private back there."

Dunk followed me out, slouching sullenly against a green dumpster. I hopped up onto some piled crates across from him, lessening my height disadvantage. Dunk reached into his back pocket and shook out a cigarette from a badly crumpled hard pack. I wasn't surprised to see he was smoking Marlboros. They could make a commercial for the damn things in this town, I thought wryly.

"So, what do you want, anyway?" he asked.

"Well, Dunk, I'm sure you're aware there's been quite a lot going on around here lately, and I'm just trying to find out where everyone was during these crimes. For example, can you tell me where you were the night before last from around nine o'clock on?"

"I didn't have nothin' to do with stealin' that liquor. Did that bitch say I did? I already told her, I spent the night at Dougie Martin's. You can ask anybody."

"Well now Dunk, I've already talked to quite a few people, and I know you didn't spend the entire evening at the Martins'. Sure you were there, and sure you came back, but in between, now that's what I want to hear about."

He glanced up at me, then resumed staring at his size fourteen tennis shoes. It should be easy to match those shoes to any prints found at the Hendersons', I thought. I'd have to talk to Sheriff Booker soon.

"I didn't go nowhere," he said. "Anyone who says I did is a damn liar."

"Do you have a boat?"

"No. Why?"

"How about Alan or Doug? I bet one of them has a boat."

"So?"

"So, I hear you guys like to take night rides sometimes, without the running lights. That true?"

"What if we do? So what?"

"I'm just wondering why you guys didn't report

that fire over at the Hendersons' when you were so close to it. Was it because you'd taken Doug's dad's boat without permission and were afraid he'd get in trouble? Is that why you didn't report the fire?"

"What makes you think we saw the fire?"

"Oh, we know you saw the fire, Dunk. That's not even in question. Plenty of people saw you out there, including me. I'm just wondering why you didn't report it. I told the sheriff just yesterday that I figured you were afraid of getting into trouble because you weren't supposed to be out in the boat."

"How could you see us? It was totally dark!" he blurted out. I let this sink in for a minute, savoring his blunder. He began taking agitated puffs of his cigarette, clearly furious at himself, or me, or both.

"So, why didn't you report the fire?"

"It's like you said. We didn't want to get in trouble for taking Mr. Martin's boat. Anyway, it was nearly out when we saw it."

"Have you ever heard the saying that if you're going to lie, you should stick as close to the truth as possible?"

He said nothing, his gaze flicking across the ground as if he were watching some invisible ping pong match.

I decided to take a plunge. "I hear it was your idea to set the fire. But somehow I don't believe it. Still, it's your word against theirs."

"No way!" he yelled, his eyes finally coming to life. Behind the dull, opaque walls of green were flecks of anger.

"Did that fucking Pinkerton tell you that? He's a goddamned liar! No way."

"They say you were all hot to trot for the older

girl. I think her name's Mary? And that you were making calls, and when her old man said he was going to call the cops, you decided to teach them all a lesson and set their house on fire."

"That's not me!" he nearly shouted. "That's Alan. I never even knew that girl. Who told you it was me? I'm gonna kick their ass!"

"So you're saying it was Alan's idea to light the fire, not yours?"

"I'm not saying nothing!" he said, realizing too late that he'd just implicated his friend.

"Look, Dunk. Let's say I believe you, and that it wasn't you who thought up the whole idea. Still, there's clear evidence that you were there. Not many people have shoes the exact same size and brand as you do, and those prints were all over the scene. So you see, it's not a question of whether or not you were there. What it's going to come down to is how cooperative you are with the police. I'd like to be able to tell Sheriff Booker that you're here to help. That's a whole lot better than being an uncooperative suspect."

He stood there blinking into the sunlight, clearly searching for a way out of his predicament. I decided not to bring up the break-in at the school or the murder. I didn't want to send him running until the sheriff or Grimes had a chance to question him. Right now I felt Dunk was primed for a big-time confession, the bulk of which would revolve around selling out his buddies. I didn't want to scare him away.

"The sheriff should be stopping by soon, Dunk. My advice to you is to be totally up front with him on this. The only thing he hates worse than a criminal, is somebody who lies to him. You definitely don't want to get on his bad side. You catch what I'm saying here, Dunk?"

He nodded slowly, the angry specks in his eyes smoldering.

I left, hoping I hadn't gone too far before Booker could get to him. I decided to give Booker a call from the pay phone in front of McGregors and let him know what I'd learned. Naturally he was out, and the best I could do was leave a brief message on his voice mail. I barely got to the part about Dunk when I was cut off. Hopefully it would be enough to get him started on interviewing the boys. I was pretty much convinced that the Three Musketeers, as Jessie called them, had been involved in the arson. I still didn't know how or even *if* it tied in with Trinidad's murder, but at least I was making progress.

I walked for about a block, trying to make up my mind about whether to head to the fort or to go back over to question Tommy. I also needed to check up on Ed Beechcomb's whereabouts Wednesday and Friday, and even though it wouldn't prove much, I was dying to get a look at Alan Pinkerton's team jacket to see if it was torn. The missing formaldehyde still had me puzzled. I'd begun to imagine all sorts of yucky things floating in glass jars. My first assumption about someone wanting to preserve Trinidad's privates may have been a little rash, but I couldn't help thinking that someone was preserving something somewhere. I thought of all those notices on the bulletin board at McGregors about lost animals and had to shake my head to get rid of the ghastly image that floated up.

While I stood on the sidewalk pondering my choices, the wail of an ambulance siren sounded out on Highway One. It approached from the south and I expected the noise to pass right on by, on its way to an accident somewhere up the highway. I was surprised when the ambulance turned into Cedar Hills and went screaming down Main Street, right past me. Right behind it came a police car, its lights and siren adding to the din. Sirens were beginning to become a regular sound in Cedar Hills. For some reason, I found myself following the sirens.

It didn't take long to catch up to them, and by the time I got there, a crowd had gathered. Along the side of the old, seldom-used road leading to North Lake, a green Cadillac had gone off the road into a ditch. The car lay on its side, and paramedics were working to free the trapped driver. I looked around for someone I knew in the crowd and spotted Tommy, shirtless under Levi's coveralls.

"What happened?" I asked, coming up beside him.

"Guy's trapped inside the Cadillac down there. Must've been there all night. Probably drunk as a skunk and run himself off the road."

"How do you know he's been there since last night?"

"On account of because his lights are still on," Tommy said, looking at me like I was an idiot.

"Oh."

"Mrs. Townsend was walking Bonkers this morning and the dog started going crazy when they got near that embankment. She could hear the guy moaning and stuff, and she run all the way back home to call the police. Me and Mr. Townsend come back here with her, but we couldn't budge the guy. He's caught purdy good by the steerin' wheel and can't get out."

"Any idea who it is?" I asked.

"Some old geezer. Never seen him before. Must have plenty of money though, be drivin' a fancy set of wheels like that. Course, it won't be worth much now. It musta rolled a couple of times before it hit bottom. It's banged up real good."

Another police car came thundering to a stop, and I was surprised to see Martha and her new partner climb out to join the others. A few minutes later, the crowd broke into cheers as an elderly man was finally freed and lifted onto a stretcher. He was clearly agitated, one arm gesticulating wildly to the officers while he was being hefted up the embankment, the other arm bent at a horrible angle. I could hear him yelling but couldn't quite make out the words.

Once the ambulance whisked him away, the crowd began to thin, and Tommy disappeared before I could question him further. I knew if I stuck around long enough, Martha would spot me and come over. I wasn't sure if I was up to talking about last night, but I still wanted to fill her in on my findings and get her opinion. As it turned out, I didn't have to wait long.

"How's my favorite detective?" she asked, flashing a contagious grin.

"Pretty good, considering. What's the story here?" I said, indicating the crash site.

"Looks like the guy got run off the road. He's madder than hell. Says he was minding his own business and this red sports car came up behind him flashing its lights, tapping his bumper, finally pushing him right off the road. It sounded pretty wild, except sure enough there's red paint on the driver's side of the car. It's amazing he wasn't hurt worse. His airbag's what saved him, but the steering column collapsed, trapping him in his seat. His left arm was broken so he couldn't reach to move the seat back. Once they figured that out, getting him out was pretty easy."

"Who is he?" I asked.

"Just a tourist, I guess. He had California plates, so I'm assuming that. Actually, I should say 'plate.' The rear one is missing."

"Was it on there before the accident?"

"How would I know, Cass? Why?"

I quickly told her my theory about the Hendersons' missing sign, the missing formaldehyde, and the possibility that whoever was committing the crimes in town was taking trophies from each crime scene.

"You telling me you think the fire and Trinidad's murder were committed by the same perp, and now this accident too? I don't know, Cass. I mean, that license plate could have been lost before. Or maybe it came off when it rolled. And besides," she went on, "what's the motive? I just don't see it. This guy was passing through. At least as far as we know. People don't just go out and randomly commit crimes like this. There's no pattern. Or if there is, I sure as hell don't see it. What's the common link between Erica's uncle, the Hendersons and this guy? Find me that and I'll buy it." I wondered vaguely if this guy had been in town long enough to meet Betty Beechcomb and shook my head.

For the first time in my life, I found myself getting really angry with Martha. I didn't have all the answers, but I at least expected her to take my questions halfway seriously.

Our conversation was interrupted by shouts about two hundred feet farther down the road. One of the officers was waving and shouting excitedly. We raced over with the others and I could finally make out what he was saying.

"There's another one down here! And it's red!"

I stood by, heart pounding, as the cops scrambled down the embankment where the crumpled body of a red Miata lay crushed against the rocks. All I could think of was Erica.

Chapter Fifteen

It was probably less than a minute before it was clear that no one was trapped inside, but it felt like an eternity. After searching the area, in case the driver had been thrown from the wreckage, most of the officers returned to the side of the road where I stood unable to move.

"There's green paint on the passenger's side of the Miata that sure looks like the color of that Caddy back there," Martha said. "I guess the man was telling the truth."

"What about the license plates?" I said.

"They're both there," Martha said, not looking at me. At least she had checked.

"Martha, I think that Miata is Erica's." I shrugged. "She's got one just like it. It's been parked at the marina and I didn't see it this morning, unless she moved it to the lodge. Do you think Erica could have —"

"Erica never left her room last night." She cut me off. "There's no way in the world she's involved in this, okay? She was still sleeping when I left her this morning."

My heart, which had been racing with anxiety, plummeted. It was as if my best friend had just sucker-punched me. "Oh," I said, "well, thank God. It must be some other Miata." My words sounded far away, as if spoken by someone else in a tunnel. I felt myself moving away, my feet going faster and faster until I realized I was running.

"Hey! Cassie, wait up!" Martha grabbed my elbow. "Slow down, damnit, you're making me look bad." I slowed to a walk, turning away from her, refusing to let her see the tears which had started to run down my face.

"Would you like to tell me what the hell's gotten into you?" she asked, tugging again at my elbow.

"Fuck off," I said, pushing her away.

There was a stunned silence.

"Fuck off?" she finally said, dumbstruck. "You're telling *me* to fuck off?" Her voice had risen at least two notches. I continued to walk, wishing she'd just turn back. She kept pace beside me, the silence between us building unbearably. At last, I stopped, and wheeled on her. "Look, this is my problem, okay? You can sleep with anyone you want to. I made a mistake, that's all. It won't happen again. I'm sorry I told you to fuck off. Let's just forget it."

Martha was staring at me, her big brown eyes looking mortally wounded.

"You think I slept with Erica? Is that it? You think I slept with the first woman you've even shown the slightest little interest in in over three years? That's what you think of your best friend?" Her voice had reached dangerous decibels and I wasn't at all sure she wasn't about to deck me.

"You just said you did." I began to cry in earnest.

"No, James. That's what you heard. That's the conclusion you jumped to. Yes, I spent the night in Erica's motel room. In fact, we drank ourselves silly. Stayed up half the night talking. About you, asshole. The woman is totally smitten. Not with me, you dumbfuck. With you." Martha was so mad her face had turned crimson and her brown eyes flashed angrily.

I stood looking at her helplessly and she turned to leave. "Please don't walk away right now," I said, my voice weak with emotion.

"You've really pissed me off here, kiddo. I'm hurt, okay?" She stood, her back to me, her fists bunched at her sides.

"I'm really sorry, Martha. I swear to you. I don't know what else to say. I'm asking you to forgive me."

She turned, and it broke my heart to see she was crying. She held her arms open and I hugged her with all the strength I had. We stood there long enough to make the passersby wonder. Long enough to earn a whistle from one of her colleagues way down the road.

Finally, I broke away. "You really talked about me?" I asked, rubbing the tears off my face with my sleeve.

"All fucking night." She grinned. "That girl has got it bad for you, babe. I just hope you get your damned act together before you screw it up. That's twice in two days you've gone off half-cocked, you know."

"I know. I'm sorry. It must be hormonal. I've spent three years ignoring the damn things and now all of the sudden they're raging out of control."

We started walking back toward the others, and I could see that our favorite person, Sergeant Grimes, had joined the other officers.

"Listen," Martha said. "You better go warn Erica that a Miata's been found and that Dickhead Grimes is on the scene. God help her if it does turn out to be hers. The registration's missing, but it won't take them long to identify it. I can vouch for her whereabouts, but I'd rather not have to. The man just lies in wait for me. If *you* jumped to the conclusion that we were sleeping together, I can just imagine what Grimes is going to think."

Feeling like a total heel, and yet at the same time strangely exhilarated, I jogged all the way to the Cedar Hills Lodge, hoping I wasn't too late to find Erica.

Chapter Sixteen

I was beginning to think I'd missed her when finally a disheveled Erica opened the door a crack, peering out with what was clearly a whale of a hangover. Her eyes were red and watery, and her hair stuck out in various directions, but she was still incredibly beautiful.

"You look like hell," I said. "What did Martha do, try to drink you under the table?"

"Thank you very much," she said, stepping aside and ushering me into the room. She shuffled back toward her bed and sat down with a plop. She caught me smiling at her and scowled. "What?" she demanded.

"You tried to outdrink her, didn't you?"

In answer, she held her head between both palms and began massaging her temples.

"I've done that a couple of times myself," I said. "It never works. Martha has an incredible capacity for food and liquor. And she never really gets drunk. Just happy. Here, let me do that."

Erica had begun rubbing her own neck and I moved behind her, using my fingers to knead the knotted muscles, massaging the tense spots, working my way to her head and back down again until I felt her finally relax. Touching her sent surges of electricity rippling through my body and I had to steady myself to keep from swaying.

"Better?" I asked.

Her answer was something between a purr and a warble.

"About last night," I started, but she reached up, her hands covering mine.

"Please don't say one word about that." She pulled me down on the bed beside her, cupping my face with her slender fingers. "You were wrong and so was I. Okay? So we're even. So let's forget it." She leaned forward and kissed me lightly on the lips. Swarms of giant butterflies took flight, threatening to make off with my heart.

"You have no idea how you make me feel," I whispered.

"Shhh," she whispered back, pulling me over on top of her. Our lips, sensuous and wet, fit together in a kiss like no other I'd experienced. Spasms of pleasure shot down my body, and I gave in to the falling sensation I'd been fighting for so long. The relief was unimaginable. Eyes closed, I searched her face with my fingers, tracing her nose, her smooth cheeks, her full lips, trailing my hands down the soft skin of her neck and sliding my hand inside the warm, terry robe.

A low moan escaped her lips as I reached her nipple, its velvety bud hard in my palm. Kissing her, my own nipples grew hard in response. I didn't want to leave her mouth, yet I found myself sliding downwards, circling her breasts with my tongue, taking first one, then the other, sucking them until she gasped.

For a moment, I feared that that was it, but Erica began to move in a way that caused me to tremble, and I knew we'd just begun.

Slowly, while we kissed, I helped her unbutton my blouse. She began to kiss my breasts, rolling me over onto my back, her fingers deftly sliding my pants down over my hips. It was clear she'd done this before but I scarcely cared, secretly praising whichever lover had taught her to move like that, down my belly toward the wetness between my legs.

She was doing to me what I'd always done to others, and whatever weak protest I might have made got lost in my own pleasure.

She was everywhere and I couldn't concentrate, I didn't want to. Her fingers slid in effortlessly, thrusting in rhythm with her own body as she straddled my leg. We moved together, unafraid, unaware of anything but each other.

What had begun as gentle lovemaking turned suddenly fierce and demanding. We were taking each other with reckless, unbridled passion. I buried myself in her, tasting the warm, tangy seawater against my tongue. I was drowning in her and did not care. She was drowning with me.

There was no part of her I did not explore, no part of me not pulsing with desire. Each time I reached what I thought was the final pinnacle, my heart hammering in my chest, my lungs gasping for air, she'd wait just a minute and then slowly, tortuously, start to move again. And again, our dance would begin.

I had never known a woman who could match me orgasm for orgasm. Never known for myself how far I could go. Erica, it seemed, was intent on breaking me, and I was not inclined to stop her.

But it was Erica who finally whispered, "Enough!" after one frenzied moment in which both of us, fingers deep inside, climaxed together. I collapsed on top of her, our sweaty bodies pressed together, our hearts thundering a percussive duet. I buried my face in her hair, breathed in the raw, sexy perfume of her skin, as content as I'd ever been.

We must have drifted off, although it couldn't have been for long. I awoke with a start at the piercing shriek of a siren shattering the calm, jerking me back into reality. I felt Erica stroking my hair, letting her long fingers slide down my cheek, my neck, circling my breast before continuing downward.

"What's wrong?" she asked when I pulled away.

"I just remembered why I came to see you."

"You mean you didn't come to seduce me?" She pulled me back toward her, her eyes laughing. I tried murmuring something about her Miata but the words got lost in a kiss so long and passionate that by the time it was over both of our bodies were again soaked in sweat, our throats hoarse from our own cries and our nerves so sensitive that the slightest touch threatened to send us straight to the highest peak again.

In the end, it was Erica who pulled us up from our incredible passion, getting out of bed for a glass of water.

"I think we've just discovered the cure for a hangover," she said, laughing.

"In that case," I replied, "let's get drunk every day."

She laughed again, her deep sexy voice spreading through me like warm syrup. "What was that you said about my Miata?" She climbed back onto the bed, handing me the glass of water which I gulped gratefully.

I forced myself to sit up. All of my muscles seemed to be in some gelatinous state, and I had to cross my arms just to hold myself together. My insides hummed but my extremities were shaky as hell. Doing my best to keep from touching her as I spoke, and failing a good deal of the time, I told her about the morning's events, starting with what I'd learned from Jess's daughter about the fort, my intimidation of Dunk at McGregors and ending with the two cars found over the embankment. After some hesitation, I also told her about my scene with Martha, which she found hilariously amusing.

"You guys had never fought before?" she asked.

"Not like that. I totally lost it."

"Because you thought she'd slept with me?" She stroked my cheek.

"Yes," I said finally. "Because I thought she'd slept with you."

159

She kissed my ear.

"I felt like my best friend was stealing from me. I kind of overreacted."

"You kind of do that," she said, kissing my cheek. "But I'm glad that's how you feel. And if I didn't have to go check to see if my car is still where I left it, I'd like to take about an hour telling you how I feel." She gave me one last kiss on my forehead and pushed herself off the bed, heading straight for the shower. I followed her.

It didn't take us long to dress, but I was surprised when I checked my watch to see how much time had passed. It was nearly three o'clock in the afternoon. Hurriedly, we left the motel room and headed for the parking lot where Erica confirmed that her red Miata was missing.

"I guess I better report it," she said sadly. "I didn't even think to set the car alarm. I just never expected that someone would steal it in Cedar Hills."

"That fool Grimes probably thinks you ran the old man off the road yourself. We've got to talk to Sheriff Booker first. I still think this is connected to the other crimes, even if Martha doesn't."

"You think whoever took it knew it was my car?" she asked. "Maybe they're trying to pin my uncle's death on me by getting me mixed up in this."

"Or maybe they've seen you and me running around together and they're trying to scare us off."

"Or maybe they just ripped off the coolest wheels in town," she said, trying hard to smile. Considering the fact her car had just been stolen, involved in a crime and then left smashed in a ditch, she was handling this very well, I thought.

"Come on," I said. "Let's run out to my place. I

want to see if Tom Booker has called me back, and I think it's probably better for you not to be seen hanging around right now. Not until we at least tell him what's happened. Otherwise, Grimes is likely to haul you back in for another polygraph."

Chapter Seventeen

It was one of those Sundays when the hot sun beat down on the blue water in shimmering waves. Sailboats, fishing boats, jet skis and speedboats sliced through the water, sending up white spray behind them. I would have loved to spend the rest of the day on the lake with Erica, taking our time, showing her the places I'd found, finding new places with her. But instead I sped toward home.

I knew someone had been there as soon as I docked, because there was water on the dock from someone's bow line. Meaning we'd just missed them. Probably the sheriff, I thought, or Sergeant Grimes.

As soon as I reached the front porch, I knew something was wrong. The sliding glass door was wide open and the cats were not there to greet me as they always did. I supposed they'd gotten out after whoever had been here had left.

Cautiously I entered, preparing myself for signs of burglary, but everything seemed in place. Walking from room to room, I tried to ignore the growing sense of dread I felt creeping up the back of my neck.

"Cass! In here!" Erica's voice from the bathroom startled me.

Across the bathroom mirror was an ugly scrawl of red spray paint, the letters dripping, still wet and shiny. "Two Less Pussies To Stroke" was the gruesome message. Below it was a large, block-style swastika and a smiley face, blood-like paint dripping from its toothless grin.

Knowing it was pointless, but unable to stop myself, I began a frantic search for Gammon and Panic. I looked under beds, in closets and outside. I called their names repeatedly, and even checked my storage shed, all the while fighting back tears. But I couldn't give in to them yet. Not while there was still a chance my kitties were alive. Those bastards had just left, and I had a good idea where they were going. I just hoped they hadn't hurt my cats. There was no doubt in my mind that the sick, Nazi-loving assholes had something demented and tortuous in mind.

Back inside, Erica waved me over to the phone

where she was rewinding my answering machine. "Cass, listen to this."

Sheriff Booker's gravelly voice came over the line. "If you're there, pick up. Well, I guess you're not. Listen, I got your message, and I want you to tread lightly. Please don't make another move until we've had a chance to talk. I've been doing a little research. You got me thinking about people who kill in groups. It's not as unheard of as you might think. Manson got people to kill for him. Others have too. Almost always, there's one real strong leader that the others look up to. Like a cult figure. In some cases, there are only two, one submissive, the other dominant. But the group can grow. Look at Jonestown and that group in Waco, Texas. And often, once the murdering starts, it's like a fire out of control. That may be what's happening here." He paused, sighing heavily. "Anyway, I talked to the Pinkerton boy, and I have to tell you, that's one scary kid. Cool one second, ready to explode the next. But so far I've got nothing concrete linking him to any of the crimes. I'm gonna go have a chat with that boy Dunk, like you suggested. One way or the other, I feel this thing is about to break wide open. By the way, the autopsy report shows Trinidad was stabbed to death, probably with the same knife that was used to sever his penis. Turns out he didn't drown at all, for what it's worth. Oh and Cass, one other thing. Betty Beechcomb called nine-one-one last night. Said her husband had gone berserk and was threatening her with a butcher knife. By the time a unit arrived, Ed Beechcomb had disappeared, and he's still missing. I told Grimes what you said about her having an affair with Trinidad, and he's put out an APB for Ed."

The long beep sounded, cutting off anything further he might have wanted to say. Well, I thought, the anger churning inside my gut, Beechcomb might well have killed Trinidad, but he sure as hell wasn't the one who had just kidnapped my cats. Suddenly, those jars of formaldehyde leaped into my mind, and my jaw clamped down so hard that I tasted blood.

I dialed the sheriff's office, and this time rather than his voice mail, I got Doris, his secretary, which surprised me since it was Sunday.

"This is Cassidy James," I said. "Is there any way I can get hold of the sheriff?"

"Oh, you're the woman detective he's been working with. I feel as though I know you, I've heard so much about you the past few days. Unfortunately the sheriff asked not to be disturbed except for dire emergencies. He's out on a case right now. I'm just here trying to catch up. We've had so much business lately! Can I take a message?"

I didn't know Doris, and in a town this small, anything I told her might well be passed along to the next person she saw. "Just have him call me as soon as he gets in," I said, and with a fury I didn't know I possessed, I stormed toward my bedroom.

Chapter Eighteen

"What are you doing?" Erica asked, following me down the hallway.

"I'm getting my jacket," I said. "Then I'm going to find that fort Jessie told me about."

"Don't you think you should wait for the sheriff, Cassie?" Worry lines etched her forehead. "He said for you to tread lightly, I heard him."

"Yeah, well, tough shit," I said, my anger unfairly coming out at Erica. I reached out and touched her cheek, silently pleading with her to understand. "I can't let them hurt my cats," I said, more softly.

"You don't know for sure that it was them," she said. The ensuing silence told us we both knew it was. "What if they're there right now? You can't just do this by yourself. These guys are sick! I really think you should wait and let the police handle it."

I reached into my closet and removed the .38 from the holster hanging next to my purse. I carried both about equally often, which was almost never. I slid the gun into the waistband of my jeans, the way Martha had taught me, letting my jacket hang over it. When I turned around, Erica was staring at me, her mouth open, eyes wide.

"Cassie, this has gone far enough. Let the police handle this." Her brow was furrowed.

"It'll be fine, Erica." I zipped up my jacket. "There's no time to wait for the police. These are my cats, and I'm going to get them."

"You're off the case," she said, blocking the doorway.

"What?"

"You heard me. I hired you and now I'm firing you. You're off the case, starting now."

"This isn't your uncle's case anymore, Erica. It's my case. Come on, step aside." Gently, I pushed her arm, but she held firm, blocking my way.

We stood looking at each other, our eyes locked. Finally, she inched over and let me pass.

"If I'm not back in two hours, call Martha and the sheriff," I said.

She followed me down the walkway to my dock. "I'm coming with you," she said.

By the look in her eyes, I knew there was no point in arguing. I may have won one staredown, but Erica Trinidad was not about to let me win this one. I hopped into my Sea Swirl and let Erica untie us. She climbed in, sat beside me, and in silence we jetted over to the county dock.

It was close to five by the time we reached town. The trickiest part was getting past everyone in town without being seen. By now the police would be looking for Erica, thinking she'd somehow been involved in the crash of her Miata, even if Grimes was busy looking for Beechcomb.

Meanwhile, it seemed everyone was out and about on this beautiful day. Pretending we were out for a leisurely stroll, we smiled and nodded as we passed familiar faces. We crossed Main Street, passing McGregors, Jess's place, the tavern, the liquor store, the doughnut shop, the defunct gas station and the church. Just past the church, we headed east, following little Jessie's directions. Clapboard houses painted green and pink dotted the tree-lined street. Dogs barked as we passed, and the sounds of televisions carried out through open front doors. Lawn mowers and weed-eaters whined, and now and then the smell of a barbecue wafted upward. This was Cedar Hills on a summer Sunday. Had I not been so worried about my cats, I might've actually enjoyed it.

Abruptly, the pavement ended, replaced by gray gravel. We clomped along, fighting for traction on the slippery surface. Soon, the gravel gave way to a dirt path, at which point I took out Jessie's map. We were probably only a half mile from town, but already we were out of earshot and sight of civilization.

"This is it here." I pointed to an old rusty beer can lodged atop a stake in the ground. We pushed our way through the thick underbrush, looking for the path Jessie had promised would emerge. I was beginning to think we'd missed it, when without warning we burst into a clearing. Sure enough, a sort of path led out of the bushes, along a dried creekbed.

"You sure you don't want to go back and call the sheriff?" Erica asked.

I took her hand, and as we walked along side by side on the narrow path, a dreadful sense of urgency pushed us forward.

I didn't need to consult the map from that point on, because the path led upward toward a huge outcropping of granite, which we could see from some distance. I was glad I was in good shape because the climb was pretty steep. When we reached the rocky hill, it was only a matter of edging around to the south, and there in front of us was the dark opening of the train tunnel. It was impossible to tell how long it was, because it curved, allowing almost no light from the other side to penetrate the blackness. The tunnel barely seemed wide enough to hold a train, let alone two additional bodies, but I eased forward, squeezing Erica's hand.

"Jesus," she whispered, her voice echoing against the granite walls. "I sure as hell hope you're right about this hardly ever being used anymore." So I had told a small fabrication. For all I knew, it was true. No point in worrying ourselves unnecessarily.

At first, the light from the opening allowed us to

see ahead, but as our eyes adjusted to the dark, so did the opening seem farther away, until soon we were using our hands against the wall to guide us. It was slow going, but we inched forward, sliding sideways like crabs, murmuring encouragement to each other as we went.

We were almost to the bend in the tunnel, nearly halfway through, when I began to sense a faint vibration at my feet. At first I thought I was imagining it, letting fear sway my imagination. But the trembling grew stronger and by the time Erica dug her nails into my hand, the ground was shaking.

Before the train even entered the tunnel, the walls began to vibrate and we pressed ourselves against them, knowing that in a few seconds the train would come hurtling toward us. An ear-splitting whistle shrieked through the darkness, and I thought Erica screamed too, but I couldn't be sure because the roar of the train was deafening.

"Hold on!" I shouted, but my voice was drowned out by the thundering, terrifying roar as the train neared. Its headlight was blinding as it rounded the bend in the tunnel, and a second later the train itself was upon us. The ground shook, threatening to topple us as the deafening din whooshed past, inches away. I could taste the burning metal, mixed with the metallic bitterness of my own fear. The heat was unbearable, hardly cooled by the terrible wind that tugged at our clothing, ripped at the skin on our faces. Slammed against the tunnel wall, we gripped each other's hands. I squeezed my eyes shut, the air sucked out of my lungs. It seemed to go on forever, and even when it had finally passed, and we were unbelievably still alive, my ears roared and my limbs trembled miserably. Neither of us moved until the tracks had quit vibrating.

Erica let go of my hand and slugged me in the arm. It hurt, but not as much as the indentations she'd left in my palm.

"I hate you!" she yelled, punching me again, not quite as hard as the first time. "You flat out lied to me, didn't you? I almost peed my pants!"

"I did pee my pants," I said. "But just a little."

She giggled at this, and soon we were both laughing. Once again, I began edging sideways along the wall, using my hands, still trembly, to feel the way. I wasn't nearly as afraid as I was before. The odds of another train coming right on the heels of the last one seemed impossible. Still, we didn't exactly dally on the way, and before we knew it, daylight came pouring through the mouth of the tunnel.

I blinked at the harsh light, glad to be out of the tunnel. My heart was still hammering and we rested for a while against a tree while I consulted Jessie's map one last time. The fort was just over a small hill to our left, but as she had said, it was completely invisible from where we stood. We listened hard, straining to hear as we tiptoed our way up the hill. Birds were all we heard, and the rustling of trees in the breeze.

"Stay here," I whispered to Erica. "Let me go first. If it's all clear, I'll come get you. If there's a problem, run like hell back to town and get help. Got it?"

"Through the tunnel?" she asked. I didn't answer and finally she nodded, her eyes wide, but clear.

Bent over at the waist, I crested the hill and

there, concealed in a stand of trees, was the fort. My pulse quickened. I stood motionless, listening and looking for any sign of activity. There was none. Cautiously, I went forward.

The fort was actually of wood construction, built by the forestry service back when this area had been logged. From the height of the new trees, I guessed it hadn't been used in over twenty years. It was a one-room building, wood plank, with windows on two sides and a rock chimney jutting out of the roof. A warm haven for the tired loggers. And a cozy hideaway for bored teens.

The glass was broken out of the windows, whether from snowstorms, birds or vandals, who could tell. But the door was still on its hinges, hanging slightly ajar. I pulled my gun from my waistband, held it in both hands skyward and kicked the door open. I counted to three and then entered, doing the standard cop crouch, aiming my gun in each direction until satisfied that the room was empty.

Well, *empty* wasn't quite the right word. The boys had made themselves quite a hangout. Boxes packed with liquor, cigarettes and food were piled high against one wall. *McGregors* was stamped on the outside of each box, and I doubted if the boys had receipts for the goods. True to form, heavy metal posters adorned the walls along with pictures of women in bondage and several pictures of Hitler giving his famed salute. Magazines were stacked in one corner, and I could easily guess their content. A crude wooden crate sat upside down in the center of the room, surrounded by beach chairs, an enormous cassette player serving as centerpiece. I took in the sordid details, but all I could hear was. my own inner voice crying, "My cats aren't here! My cats aren't here!"

I'd been so sure that it was the boys who'd taken my cats, and that they'd brought them here. I'd even gone so far as to imagine jars of formaldehyde with other people's pets floating within. I'd thought if I could only get here fast enough, I'd be in time to save my kitties. Now, I wasn't sure what to do.

I turned to go, stifling a sneeze that had been building since I'd entered. The room was musty, but there was something else. An unpleasant, chemical odor. Something familiar. Suddenly my heart leaped into overdrive. The odor I kept smelling *was* formaldehyde!

I circled the room, searching, peeking into the fireplace, looking in boxes, coming up with nothing. Had they moved it? Had I scared them off with my poking around? I stared, thinking hard, then focused on the large, framed poster of Adolf Hitler on the wall. None of the other pictures had frames. They were simply affixed to the wall with tacks. But the giant Hitler was much sturdier, and the thick pine frame stood out from the wall. I moved closer and noticed that the formaldehyde odor got stronger as I approached. Carefully, I lifted the picture off the two nails holding it in place. Behind it was a recessed cupboard with three open shelves. And on the shelves lay enough hard evidence to put someone away for a long time.

Amid the carefully laid out treasures were several California license plates, the Hendersons' missing sign, some drivers' licenses, a wallet and a yearbook photo of a girl whom I recognized as having disappeared earlier that summer. She'd been assumed to be a runaway at the time, but seeing her photo next to the other items, I doubted she was still alive.

The objects seemed to be grouped, but not in any pattern I could recognize. Here and there were not one but several jars of formaldehyde, one with the lid off, which was probably why I had smelled it. The first jar held something the size of my fist, and when I drew closer, I nearly heaved. Bobbing just beneath the surface was the perfectly preserved head of a blue point Siamese. Thinking of my own cats, I noticed that a number of the jars were still empty, awaiting their own sick treasures, and I felt the knot in my stomach tighten. As repulsed as I was, I could not help examining the other jars, some containing unrecognizable blobs of what looked like flesh. When I came upon the final jar, I drew no pleasure from the realization that I had been right about the last remains of Walter Trinidad. There, suspended in clear liquid, was the small, shriveled appendage that Betty Beechcomb had disdained. The gagging sensation I'd been fighting for some time had finally surfaced, and I feared if I didn't get fresh air immediately, I might pass out right there.

"Find what you're looking for?" I turned to face the sneering blue eyes of Alan Pinkerton, his large frame blocking the doorway. He held a large cardboard box in his arms. Without any hesitation, I raised the .38 and aimed it at a point just between those devilish eyes. His response was not what I expected. He laughed.

Chapter Nineteen

"You've been a busy boy, Alan," I said, trying to keep my hand from shaking. I noted with little satisfaction that his jacket had a small tear in the sleeve. "Put your hands in the air, now."

Instead, he took several steps toward me, his smile even more frightening than his eyes. "Just a sec." He set the large box down, removed the lid and reached into it, which caused a chorus of piteous mews. My heart lurched as he stood up holding Panic in one beefy hand, Gammon in the other. His thick fingers circled their fragile necks and he held them out at arm's length, so that their wildly flailing claws batted the air. He laughed again, and tightened his grip around their necks, which caused them to quit meowing, their eyes open wide in terror.

My hand shook as I tightened my finger on the trigger.

"Now, Alan. It doesn't make much difference to me whether I shoot you here and then wait for the sheriff, or whether I let you live until he gets here. It's your choice. Put the cats down and get your fucking hands in the air!"

He raised both arms, closing his hands around the cats' necks even tighter and twirled them in the air, sashaying his hips, imitating a pompom girl. He inched toward me and I lowered my gun, aiming below the waist. I had never wanted to hurt anyone before, let alone kill. But at that moment I knew I was capable of murder.

"Put the gun down, bitch, nice and slow," came a voice from the doorway. Jess's son, Doug, stood in the entrance, his right hand holding a gun which he pressed against Erica's temple, his left hand roughly cupping her breast.

"Now!" he screamed. "Drop it!" I leaned over and laid my gun on the floor, kicking it away from me. It skidded across the wooden floor and came to rest against the boxes of liquor.

"Dougie," I said. "Let her go. She's not part of this. She hasn't seen anything. She doesn't even live here. She's leaving town today." It was hard to keep the trembling out of my voice.

"Gonna be kinda hard to do, on account of she's missing her fancy little car," Pinkerton said, laughing. Gammon and Panic had begun to pant. Erica shot him a dangerous look but I could tell she was terrified. So was I.

"Dougie, don't get in any more trouble than you're already in," I said, grasping at straws. "The sheriff knows Pinkerton's behind all this. Let him take the fall. Right now, you're merely an accessory. You're not even eighteen yet. They'll go easy on you."

Doug's laugh was harsh, ugly. More of a snort than a laugh. "Pinkerton's in charge, is he? Since when? Is that what you think? Shit, you're dumber than he is."

I looked back and forth between Doug and Alan, realizing too late that Jess's son was the ringleader of this little group. Alan was staring at him with something akin to awe. He'd just been called dumb and he was gazing at his accuser like a loyal dog.

"Okay," I said, trying to appease him. "I can see now that you're the boss. That's all the more reason for you to quit now, before somebody else gets hurt."

"Somebody else gets hurt," Pinkerton mimicked in a high falsetto, twirling the cats near my face. From the pained expression on their faces, I knew Pinkerton was close to choking them to death.

"Put those damn things down," Doug ordered. "Let's take these bitches out and do 'em, right now."

Alan carefully, almost lovingly placed the cats back in the cardboard box. I noticed he had a sheathed knife on his belt. "Good little pussy cats," he murmured, closing the lid. "You wait right here. Later, we have a fun little game we're going to play. You like fireworks, don't you?" He stood up and walked to the exposed shelves, placing the box next to the Hendersons' sign and one of the license plates.

It suddenly dawned on me how they had organized the objects. The license plate and the Hendersons' sign were Alan's. These were his crimes and his trophies. I looked at the box and shuddered to think that Gammon and Panic would be his next victims.

I looked quickly at the largest pile which held the photo of the missing girl, several more license plates, the jar holding Trinidad's penis and something nailed to a board that looked dismayingly like a severed nipple. I walked over, hoping they couldn't tell how badly my knees were shaking, and picked up the glass jar.

"This must be your work, eh, Dougie? The biggest pile of all. I guess you have to set an example for the others. Looks like Dunk is falling behind."

"Put that down," Doug said, shoving Erica into the room, the gun muzzle still pressed against her head.

I shook the jar, feigning interest in the swirling motion of the severed penis. "Why him?" I asked. "Or was he just a random victim like the others?"

"I told you to put it down," he said. He had obviously bonded with this particular treasure. I detected definite emotion in his voice.

"I'll put it down," I said, "just as soon as you tell me why. You owe us that much, anyway. After all, he was Erica's uncle."

"The bastard was a prick!" Doug said, his voice rising.

"And now that's all that's left of him! One itsy bitsy prick," Alan said, giggling. This was an interesting side of Alan Pinkerton. He was almost giddy with excitement. His close-set eyes sparkled. I liked him better the other way, surly and mean. This way, he seemed crazier than hell.

"What'd he do to make you so mad, Dougie. Mad enough to stab him. Mad enough to cut off his penis?"

"Go ahead, Dougie, tell her," Pinkerton said.

"I told you not to call me that," Doug said, threateningly. "My name is Doug. Not Dougie. Doug. You got it?" Alan nodded, his good mood somewhat diminished. "Anyway," Dougie went on, "I guess it doesn't matter now. The asshole called us a bunch of faggots. That's all. He pissed me off. He shouldn't have done that. People who piss me off can get hurt. Like you, for example. You're starting to piss me off a lot. Now put the fucking jar back down, right now!"

I gently placed the obscene container back in Dougie's pile.

"Okay, so he made you mad," I said. "But Trinidad was a big man. No offense, Dougie, but you're kind of on the short side. How'd you do it?"

Doug puffed his chest out, his face reddening at the insult. "I used my brain, that's how. I ripped off the asshole's wallet. Then I called him up, told him I'd found his wallet and wanted to return it. I had him meet us out on Cedar Point. He pulled up in his putrid turquoise boat and got out to meet me on the fishing rock. I handed him his wallet and the first thing he did was check to see if his money was there. What a jerk! Like I'm going to call him and return his wallet after stealing his money! Anyway, he had the fucking nerve to hand me a one-dollar bill as a reward! I played it perfect though. I acted all

179

grateful and when he turned to go, that's when I stabbed him. You shoulda seen the look on his face when he turned around. Only took me two stabs, too. Of course, it would have been better if he'd still been alive when I took his prick. Even so, it was pretty awesome."

I tried to keep my composure. He wouldn't be confessing if he believed we'd still be alive to tell the sheriff all this. Even so, I wanted to keep him talking. "What about the boat, Dougie. Why'd you return it?"

"For fun," he said. "To throw people off. I didn't really figure he'd be found so soon."

"Then why did you go back into his house?" I asked, doing anything to stall for time.

"Oh, that. If I'd have known then that this one here" — he patted Erica's breast almost lovingly — "was in the house, I'd have done her too. Actually, we were looking for money. The bastard was always waving it around in people's faces, I figured he'd have some stashed somewhere. But we never found shit. I was real careful to leave things nice and neat. Anything else you want to know?" His smirk told me he didn't care how long I stalled. In the end, he'd do as he pleased. Inside their box high on the shelf, my kitties had begun to meow again and my heart ached in agony.

"I understand about the Hendersons' place," I said, hiding my pain. "Alan was mad at Mary for not going out with him. But why the old man in the Cadillac? What could he have done to hurt you?"

"You still don't get it, do you?" he asked, sneering. "Californians are fair game."

"You ran him off the road because he was a Californian?" I asked, incredulous.

"He was driving too slow. Me and Alan had just borrowed your girlfriend's car. It wasn't like it was locked or anything. Thought we'd take it for a little spin then dump it somewhere, let her know she wasn't that welcome in town. But then that fat fucker wouldn't pull over and let us pass, and so we got him good. It was actually Alan's idea to dump the Miata up the road. Who knows? Maybe they'd think she'd done the whole thing. It doesn't really matter, though, does it?"

"If he'd been from some other state, would you have driven him off the road?" I asked, still having trouble with the concept.

"I could have. But would I have? Who knows? But only Californians count. Like poor Leslie there." He pointed to the photo of the missing girl. "I got no points for that one. She just pissed me off. Still, I like to look at her picture. Kinda pretty, like your friend here. Of course, she wasn't so pretty once I got through with her. That's her little titty there up on my shelf." Saying this, he squeezed so hard on Erica's breast that she gasped. Then he laughed. "Come on, Alan, you lead the way. Let's take these girls to the fire ring, do 'em there. Oh, and here. I brought you your candy." Doug tossed Alan a small, clear plastic baggie, and I watched with interest as Alan eagerly dipped the long nail of his pinky into the white powder, scooping it into first one nostril and then the other, snorting deeply. I wondered what kind of drug Dougie had Alan on. Cocaine, most likely, but it could have been crack or any number of mood-altering substances. Whatever it was, I was sure it helped keep Alan in Doug's control.

Newly recharged, Pinkerton squared his shoulders, obviously taking seriously the job of leading the way. Doug motioned for me to follow, and he brought up the rear with his gun still pressed firmly against Erica's temple.

"One funny move and this one's history," he said to me. I nodded, and turned to follow Alan who was impatiently waiting to lead our little parade. As I did so, I caught a movement out of the corner of my eye. Pretending to stretch the muscles in my neck, I tried to get a glimpse of whatever it was I'd seen, but it had vanished from sight.

Alan led us away from the fort, through thick underbrush, to a clearing in the woods. There, perched on a mound, was a large fire pit surrounded by stones.

"Undress," Doug ordered, taking the gun away from Erica's temple long enough to wave it at me. "Both of you."

Erica and I looked at each other and slowly began unbuttoning our blouses. Her eyes smoldered with anger, and I feared she would do something stupid. As best I could, I tried to calm her down with my own eyes, but her anger was palpable. .

"I heard my dad say you were a dyke," Doug said. He turned and spit on the ground. "Guess you just been waiting for the right man to come along, huh?"

"I can't imagine your father using that word," I replied.

"Actually, you're right. He said something like 'She's of the lesbian persuasion.' As far as I'm concerned, you're a cunt-fucking dyke. Take off your pants."

As I undid my shoelaces, I caught a movement in the bushes behind Doug, and this time I saw the briefest glint of metal before the shape disappeared again. Someone was out there with a gun, that much I was sure of. Was it Dunk? My heart skipped a beat thinking maybe, just maybe it was Sheriff Booker, or better yet, Martha. But the figure was too tall for either of them, I thought, my hopes sinking. And besides, no one else even knew this fort existed, let alone that we were out here.

Face it, Cassidy, I told myself, there's no one here to save you, and there's not a damn thing you can do as long as Dougie has that gun on Erica. If only I could think of a way to distract him, and somehow get the gun away from him, I thought. I'd just have to bide my time and wait for a chance to act.

"Hurry up!" Pinkerton said, coming up behind me and kicking me in the back. The force of it knocked me over and when I looked up at him, his hand was down his pants, kneading himself into erection.

"Go ahead," Doug said. "You do that one first. I'll save this one for last. Then we can switch." He grabbed Erica's exposed breast, squeezing hard, and when she slapped his hand away, he struck her across the face with the butt of his gun, drawing blood from her nose and knocking her to the ground.

Alan's eyes narrowed in excitement and he unzipped his jeans, exposing an abnormally large erection. He stood over me, waving it above me. A thin thread of spittle hung from his open mouth.

"Drop it right there!" a deep, angry voice bellowed. We all looked up to see Jess Martin step from behind a tree. He was pointing a long, double-barrel shotgun at his son. Despite his obvious anger, his voice trembled and his legs shook, and I knew exactly how he felt.

"Doug!" I yelled. "It's all over. Put down your gun!"

"Shut up," he snarled at me. "Go ahead and turn around, Dad. Run, just like you did in Vietnam. I know all about your dishonorable discharge. How you refused to shoot the fucking commie gooks. You were a coward then and you're a fucking coward now!"

"That's enough, son," Jess said, his voice steely, his gun leveled at Dougie's head.

Dougie's voice was sarcastic. "Son? What a joke! I'm not your son. No father of mine woulda wimped out on his country like you did. I don't know who my real father is, but I sure as shit know he's not a faggot like you!"

"I said that's enough, Doug. Put down the gun." Jess's voice began to waver.

"Or what?" Dougie sneered, turning the gun away from Erica to aim it at his father. The two stood, not twenty feet apart, their guns pointed at each other. Jess's hands shook, and Dougie laughed cruelly.

"I'll give you to the count of three, Daddy-o. You can turn and walk out, or you can shoot. But on the count of three, if you're still here, you're a dead man. One!"

"Don't do it, Doug," I pleaded. I noticed with some horror that Pinkerton was continuing to massage himself during this entire exchange.

"Two!" Doug yelled, steadying the gun with both hands.

"For God's sake!" I shouted. "He's your father! Let him go!" Doug didn't so much as flinch, but his thick lips curled into a hideous smile.

"Three!" he said. The roar of simultaneous blasts split the air, throwing debris in all directions. Blood erupted, gushing upward like a geyser, spewing brain matter and tissue skyward. Doug's body was thrown backward, landing in a heap in the fire pit. Across from him, Jess stood, still poised to shoot, his mouth open in shock as he watched his son torn apart by someone else's bullet.

Little Jessie stepped out from behind a bush, my revolver clutched tightly in her small, trembling fists. Her eyes were wide with terror as she walked slowly toward the fire pit, the gun still pointed at her brother's body. When she'd made absolute certain that he wouldn't be getting up again, she placed the gun on the ground, looked up at me with a bewildered frown and fainted.

I sensed more than saw Pinkerton make his move. The shimmer of metal caught my eye as he lunged, a butcher knife extended in his right hand, his massive body lurching toward the gun. I kicked out sideways, catching him squarely in the crotch. He hadn't had time to pull his pants up and the damage of the contact was both immediate and apparent. He doubled over, cupping himself, his right hand still clutching the knife. His pale, watering eyes were livid, the tiny pupils nearly invisible. Before he could lunge again, I grabbed my gun and aimed it at his midsection.

"Put that away," I said, barely suppressing a rage that welled inside me. Pinkerton must have read my face because he tossed the knife aside and, whimpering like a child, gingerly tucked his limp penis back inside his pants.

Chapter Twenty

We stood outside the fort, no one feeling like being inside with the gruesome collection. After Erica and I had gotten all our clothes back on, I'd retrieved Gammon and Panic, and we were taking turns soothing them while Jess held his daughter. We had tied Pinkerton to a tree, and now and then we could hear his whimpering, as if from some wounded, rabid beast. Pinkerton, apparently, was crying.

Jess put Jessie on the ground, covering her with his jacket, and let her sleep. She'd awakened from fainting, told us she was tired and wanted to sleep for a while longer, and then sank back down into oblivion. Her pulse and breathing were fine, but the three of us watched over her carefully.

"She's in shock," Jess said. "I just hope to God she comes out of this all right."

I put my arm around Jess and led him a little farther away from Jessie, so our voices wouldn't wake her. The day had turned to dusk and the evening air was chilly. I longed to be back home, sitting in front of the fire with Erica, or better yet, snuggled warm in bed. But Jess had told us that Sheriff Booker was on his way, and we decided to wait until he arrived.

"You okay?" I asked, reaching out and taking Jess's hand.

He shrugged, reaching for one of his cigarettes, his hands trembling. His eyes were red-rimmed, and he looked ten years older than he had that morning.

"If I'd known she was there, I'd have shot him. I never, never would have let my baby girl have to go through something like this." His voice was ragged with pain. There was so much that needed to be said, and no really good way to say it. Erica and I stood by, telling him there was no way he could have known she was there, but our words bounced off him, his grief too thick to penetrate.

Finally, Erica said, changing the subject, "How did you know to come here? And how do you know the sheriff is on his way?"

"He came by the house a while ago to see if Doug was home, and I knew there was trouble. I told him what Cass had told me this morning about the fire, and he confided to me that Dunk had pretty much told him the whole story. He said Dunk was going to lead them to some fort in the woods where the boys had stashed evidence from crimes they'd committed. The sheriff said he was going to wait for some backup, then head on out there."

His voice picked up strength as he spoke, and I squeezed Erica's hand, letting her know she'd done the right thing to ask.

"Right after the sheriff left," Jess went on, "I saw you two in town. I was going to catch up with you, to tell you what he'd said, but then I could tell by the way you were moving that you were on to something. I can't say I knew for sure that you were headed for the fort, but I had a bad feeling about the whole thing. It was like I had a premonition, because the hairs on the back of my neck stood straight up. That happened to me once in Nam and it saved my life, so I don't take it lightly when it happens now. It's true what Dougie said about me in Nam, you know. One day I woke up and I couldn't kill anymore. I absolutely couldn't do it. I can't even count how many lives I'd taken, and then all of a sudden one day, I freeze up. I can't tell you what I went through after that. But none of it compares to today. Not even close."

Jess's eyes had a faraway look that scared the shit out of me. He had wandered off the subject, and I was afraid we might not get him back. Gently, I patted his shoulder.

"What happened after you saw us go by, Jess?" I asked.

His eyes narrowed in concentration, and I could tell he was struggling to stay in the present. Then his eyes cleared, and I heaved a sigh of relief. "Anyway, I wrapped a big towel around the shotgun that Bonnie insists we keep in the house, even

189

though she knows how I feel about guns, and I took off after you. I almost lost you a couple of times, because I was trying to stay back. I damn near had a coronary when that train came tearing through the tunnel. I thought you'd both bought the farm. I had no idea that while I was following you, little Jessie was following me. She must have found your gun in the fort and followed your voices to the fire pit. If I had only known she was there, I'd have shot him myself. But I just didn't believe that Doug would actually fire on me. But he did, didn't he? And now my baby girl has killed her own brother. How's a little kid supposed to live with something like this? Can you tell me that?" His voice finally broke and he doubled over, holding his sides. Sobs racked his body, and he held onto his ribs, shaking as he cried. I put my hand on him, wishing there were words for something like this. But if there were, I didn't know them, and so I comforted him in silence while he suffered.

After what seemed an eternity, his sobs turned to deep sighs, and he was finally able to quit shaking. He lit another cigarette and we stood huddled in the growing darkness, listening to the frogs, watching over Jessie as she slept.

We could hear them before we saw them. First came Dunk, his gangly, stoop-shouldered frame leading the sheriff up the hill toward the fort. Behind the sheriff was Sergeant Grimes and the two uniformed cops that had been with him that first day on Walter Trinidad's dock. They had their guns drawn, but when they saw us clustered at the top of the hill, they holstered them and hurried up to where we stood.

We took turns telling the story, showing them the fort, leading them to Pinkerton who had finally quit whimpering, eventually taking them to Doug's body. Grimes bagged my gun and I knew it would probably be a long time before I saw it again.

It was nearly dark and a gentle breeze raised goosebumps on my arms, even though I had a jacket. Erica was shivering, and I put my arm around her for warmth. This drew a scowl from Grimes, but I couldn't have cared less. When it was clear we'd done all we could to help, I told Sheriff Booker we were going to head back. He walked us to the top of the hill and handed us his flashlight.

"Cassidy James," he said, putting his arm around my shoulders. "There are several things I'd like to say to you. First off, I like you. You don't let a hardass like Grimes get to you, and that takes *cojones*. I like girls with *cojones*. Makes 'em more interesting." His blue eyes twinkled with mischief and he winked at Erica.

I figured I could give the sheriff a lesson on feminism later. I wasn't a girl and I definitely didn't have any *cojones,* but I knew what he meant.

"Second," he went on, "I'd like to apologize for not taking you a little more seriously at first. You've certainly proven yourself to me, and even that dipshit Grimes is trying to figure out how you beat him to the punch. And lastly," he said, his voice turning serious, "the next time I ask you to tread lightly, please do me a favor and listen. This here's a small enough town that neither one of us has to be the Lone Ranger. And I definitely do not want to find you lying dead somewhere, and have to go around the rest of my life feeling guilty about it. *Capiche?*"

For answer, I stood on my tiptoes and kissed his deeply tanned cheek, which even in the waning light I could tell took on a reddish hue.

"*Capiche,*" I said.

Using his flashlight, I led Erica back down the hill, carrying the cardboard box with Panic and Gammon through the terrible tunnel, around the underbrush, down the streets of Cedar Hills, across the darkened waters of Rainbow Lake, toward home.

Chapter Twenty-one

Outside, the sun sparkled like gold and silver glitter on the water while birds dove and fished in the morning light. It was past eleven, but we were still in bed, snuggled beneath the sheets, occasionally glancing out at the view. It had been a week since that day at the fort, and once we'd finished with the necessary depositions and paperwork, and arranged for Trinidad's body to be sent back to L.A., we'd spent most of that time right where we were, now and then venturing out into the kitchen for a light meal or a glass of wine, sometimes making it as far as the hot tub or the front deck, but never straying too far from each other.

We were wrapped in each other's arms, both cats snuggled between us, when the unmistakable whir of a motorboat approached. I eased myself up on one elbow and peeked out. To my delight it was Martha.

We watched as she tied up, then lifted a large wicker picnic basket out of her boat. She was wearing white shorts and a brightly colored Hawaiian shirt, her untanned skin already pink from the ride over. Leaning over the side of the bed, I picked up Erica's shirt and handed it to her, then pulled my own shirt on over my head. It was only Martha, I mused. No point in actually getting up out of bed.

"Anybody home?" she asked, cupping her hands against the windowpane of my bedroom to peer in at us from the front porch. I wiggled my fingers at her and she flashed a grin, letting herself in the front door. A moment later, she was standing at the foot of the bed, smiling down at us, still holding the wicker basket.

"I thought maybe you two had died up here. Phone off the hook? I mean, honestly, have you even gotten out of that bed this week?"

"Once," I said. "To go to the bathroom." We all laughed, and Martha began taking things out of her basket.

"I'm here on a mission to save you from yourselves," she said. "First, sustenance, since I doubt you've been taking adequate nourishment." With this she whisked out a bottle of Mumms' Champagne, which she expertly uncorked, pouring three crystal glasses nearly full. She handed us each a glass and raised hers in a toast.

"To new friends. And old ones too." She winked at me.

We sipped the icy Champagne, letting the bubbles tickle our noses while I watched as she pulled out croissants, a plate of grapes and sliced pears, a small brick of sharp cheddar and another of Oregon blue cheese, a small tin of pâté and finally, small chocolate truffles wrapped in paper. We set this feast on the bed between us, moving Gammon and Panic to the floor, despite their protests. I broke off a bit of cheddar to appease them, but they both turned tail and huffed from the room.

"I should have brought sardines," Martha said, settling into a cross-legged position on the end of the bed facing us.

At our request, she caught us up on the world and local news while we ate. She told us that Jess and Jessie had gone off camping to spend some time together after going through all the necessary depositions. Luckily, the D.A. had decided there was no justification for pressing charges against little Jess, and apparently even Grimes agreed. Bonnie, Jess's wife, had gone to visit her mother, unable to accept or deal with what had happened. Martha told us Pinkerton had been temporarily placed in a juvenile facility up in Portland. It looked like he was so full of cocaine and steroids that it was going to take a while just to get him detoxed. At the very least, he'd be doing serious time in a youth facility, and if they tried him as an adult, it could be for much longer. Dunk, it turned out, had played only a minor role in the crimes and would probably end up doing a little time in the juvenile detention center where he was now.

"What about Ed Beechcomb?" I asked, biting off a small chunk of cheese.

"Oh, he's back in town. Betty refused to press charges, even after he kicked her out of the house for good. It seems that when he demanded that she tell him the truth about a rumor he'd heard in town, she didn't know when to stop. I guess the list went on and on. Ed just lost it. Anyway, I feel more sorry for him than her. She's already off to greener pastures. Rumor has it, little Tommy Green is in a real funk over the whole thing."

"And Cass was ready to read him his rights," Erica teased, elbowing my ribs gently.

"Oh, and the family whose house burned down?" Martha went on, sipping her Champagne, "They've decided to rebuild their house. They say the people of Cedar Hills have been so nice to them in their hour of need that they can't bear the thought of going anywhere else. By the way, I picked up your mail from the dock, in case you're interested."

Amid the bills and junk mail was a pink envelope with my address neatly printed in small, precise handwriting. The return address read simply "Jessie." I tore open the envelope and began reading the letter aloud.

"Dear Cass: After what we've been through, I felt Miss James would be kind of formal. I hope you don't mind. Dad said I should write to you to let you know that we're okay. We're camping by a river in Washington, and it seems like all we do is hike and fish. Mostly we talk and boy do we talk! Dad says you were real worried about me, but I'm fine. It's Dad who's been having a tough time. He keeps going over and over the fact that he couldn't pull the trigger and that because of that, I had to. After this vacation we're both going to start seeing a therapist from Kings Harbor named Maggie. Your cop friend, Martha, got us an appointment with her before we left and she's real nice. She reminds me a lot of you, only older I think."

I smiled, then continued reading. "Anyway, the way I explained it to Dad was like this. Being able to shoot Dougie wouldn't have made Dad any braver. Dad believed right up to the end that Dougie would come to his senses. Dad doesn't understand how a person can be bad. That's how we're different. I knew Dougie was bad. I wasn't brave for shooting Dougie. It's just that right then and there, with him having the gun on first Erica and then Dad, I was the only one who could stop him. And one thing I know for sure, Dougie had to be stopped. I still cry all the time, but I don't feel guilty. Just sad. Remember when I told you I wanted to be a cop? Dad says that's because I have an inner drive to do good, and to stop the bad guys. Now that Dougie's gone, you'd think I'd be less driven that way, but actually if anything, I feel like maybe being a cop is what I'm supposed to do. Does that sound crazy? I hope not, because I want to ask you a favor."

I took a sip of Champagne, wondering what she wanted. "Do you think when we get back I could maybe tag along on some of your investigations? I know I'm only ten, but I turn eleven next month and as you've seen, I'm not a baby anymore. I could be pretty helpful if you give me a chance, so please, think it over. Well, I better go now. Dad's down by the river screaming his head off for the net because he thinks he's hooked Moby Dick. The last one was about three inches. Oh well. See you soon."

For some reason I couldn't explain, tears had welled up in my eyes and I'd had trouble getting through the last lines. Little Jess was going to be all right, I kept thinking as I read. Everyone is going to be all right.

Erica squeezed my hand and raised her glass.

"To rookie detectives," she said, her sexy blue eyes smiling irresistibly. We all three clinked glasses and as I sipped the Champagne, I knew that sometimes it truly was good to be alive.

LOOKING FOR NAIAD?

Buy our books at
www.naiadpress.com

or call our toll-free number
1-800-533-1973

or by fax (24 hours a day)
1-850-539-9731